Plus

1

By: Erica Lee

Dedication

Dedicated to Megan. Thank you for all of the support you have always shown me throughout our friendship, especially recently with my writing. Thanks for encouraging me as I wrote this and for pushing me to see it through. Also, a special thanks for making sure I kept the characters' names the same throughout the book.

Prologue

"So are you ready?" I looked over to see Jenny's big brown eyes already staring at me. Those were the eyes that first attracted me to her and they still had the habit of taking my breath away, even though I knew they shouldn't. Her eyes always had such a nice shimmer to them, only today they didn't. Today they just looked sad. It killed me to see them looking that way. All I wanted to do was reach out and grab her hand. I wanted to tell her that everything would be ok. I wanted to promise that we would find a way to make things better. More than anything, I just wanted to make her smile again.

Instead I shrugged my shoulders and forced a fake smile onto my face. I threw on a pair of sunglasses and as the music started, I took her hand and broke into our choreographed entrance, hoping no one would realize just how broken up I was inside.

Chapter 1: 5 Years Earlier

I stood at the bar, staring out at the dance floor and studying the crowd. When the bartender handed me my drink, I nodded and gave him a tip, then promptly turned my gaze back to the dance floor. The dance floor which happened to be completely empty at this point. I sighed to myself. This wedding was definitely going to be a challenge for me. I was only 24, but had already developed a reputation as the "fun wedding guest." In the past few years, I had averaged about three weddings a year, which is unusual for someone my age. It's not as unusual when you're from a town as small as mine though. Everyone seems to get married early, mostly because they have nothing else to do. I started out with weddings of a few close high school friends, but now it seemed everyone's fourth cousin twice removed was inviting me to their weddings. What can I say? I'm a good time. I know how to get a party started and how to keep people dancing all night, so people liked having me around. I knew I had a reputation to live up to, so I took it upon myself to take the time at the beginning of every wedding reception to study the crowd and decide on my tactic to make it a fun night.

This particular wedding was for my 19 year old

cousin, Valerie, who was marrying her 21 year old high school sweetheart, John. That's where the challenge came in. Half of the people attending this wedding couldn't even drink; a lot were still in high school since my cousin had just graduated a year ago. Most of the people who could drink were choosing not to. I was actually shocked that they even had alcohol since Valerie and John were so religious. Neither of them had drank a lick in their life, even John who legally could now. I never questioned why they were getting married so young. I knew exactly why. They were both saving themselves for marriage. People saving themselves always got married young. It's not like they were any less needy than the rest of us. They just needed a label to feel ok about it. I would never understand that mindset, but oh well. To each their own.

Now don't get me wrong. I adored my cousin. She was the definition of what a Christian should be - loving, selfless, and non-judgemental. She didn't even flinch when I came out to her a few years ago. She told me that she knew I was born this way and that God loved me no matter who I loved. She is actually the reason that I now believe in God. I can totally get down with a God that is as loving as the one she talks about. I just can't give up drinking and pre-marital fun, which is where Valerie and I differ.

My thoughts were getting me off task so I tried to force myself to focus on the challenge in front of me. Just as I was about to turn to the bartender to ask for another drink, I caught someone coming up beside me out of the corner of my eye. When I felt a hand land lightly on my shoulder, I turned so I could face the perpetrator completely. As I looked into the eyes of the girl standing next to me, I felt my heart skip a beat. I never understood that expression until this very moment, but believe me, it actually happens. What drew me in were those eyes. They were brown just like mine, but while mine had that dull poop color, hers had a shimmer. It was a shimmer that caused you to get lost as you tried to define just what color it was. It was a shimmer that was currently causing me to stare blankly at her like a complete idiot, which wasn't like me at all.

She giggled and gave my shoulder a light squeeze. "Sorry if I scared you. I was told that I'm supposed to talk to you. Apparently we would get along well."

I did a quick sweep of her body trying to be discreet incase she was a friend from church who would be weirded out by another female blatantly checking her out. She was wearing a green dress that fell right above her knees and hugged her in all the right places. Her brown curly hair fell halfway down her back and when she smiled, a dimple formed on her right cheek. Simply put, she was gorgeous. She was probably one of the most beautiful females I had ever laid eyes on and I was still unable to find my voice.

I shook myself free of those thoughts. What was wrong with me? This wasn't like me. I was Rory Montgomery for God's sake. It was no secret to me that girls flock to me. My hair wasn't nearly as luscious as the mystery woman standing in front of me, but girls seemed to appreciate my shoulder length straight brown hair that I lightened with streaks of blonde highlights. They also went nuts for my subtle chin dimple. Yes, I had a slight indent in my chin that I always hated growing up. That was until I got to college and realized it was lesbian bait. But what really attracted the females was what seemed to be escaping me at the moment - my smooth talking abilities. I wasn't fake or an expert on saying the right things to get someone to melt at my words. I was a charmer. It just came naturally to me. People always told me that I was exactly like my dad. I guess his charming personality explained why I still adored him, even though he was almost never around. He moved to California when he and my mom divorced right after I graduated from high school and I had only seen him a handful of times since then. But somehow his warm embraces, sincere apologies, and promises to do better always wiped away any anger I felt toward him.

Ok.. now my mind was just going all over the place. Where was I? Oh yeah. Beautiful girl standing right in front of me. I leaned back, placing both elbows on the bar and raised a seductive eyebrow at her.

"Oh yeah?" I said with a smile. "And why is that? Does it have something to do with our dashingly good looks?"

She laughed, shaking her head at my joke and I couldn't help but notice how she slowly traced her fingers down my arm, before placing her hand on the bar beside me. That definitely didn't seem like the move of one of Valerie and John's overly friendly church friends. That was the move of a very skilled flirt.

She smiled over at me, her right dimple on full display. "It could be that, but I also think it might be the fact that we are the only two people at this wedding who are over 21 that don't have a date."

I looked around me then shrugged my shoulders. "Guilty."

"So, why doesn't a pretty girl like yourself have someone with you?" The mystery woman asked while motioning for the bartender to refill our drinks.

I stared up at the ceiling for a few beats before

answering. "I guess you could say I'm kind of a serial dater and serial daters don't get plus ones to weddings, even if it is a family wedding."

At this, the gorgeous brunette placed her elbow on the bar and put her chin in her hand, then smiled up at me. "Serial dater, huh? So why were you refused a date? Your family isn't a fan of snap crackle and pop?"

I couldn't help but laugh. This girl was witty, but two could play at that game. "Not quite. It turns out Snap and Crackle have been pretty hot and heavy for a few years now, but recently Crackle and Pop have been having a thing on the side. I'm not quite sure where I fit into that equation, but no one wants that kind of drama at their wedding."

"That's too bad," she shot back. "I've always been more of a Tony the Tiger girl myself."

I gave her a half smile, demonstrating my doubt. "Is that so?"

She slowly shook her head. "Nope. I made it up. He's not my type."

"Wrong species?"

"Wrong gender."

I tried to keep a goofy grin from spreading across my face from her confirmation. Instead I pointed one finger in the air like I just had a revelation.

"Aha. So that's why they said we would get along. The only two lesbians at this wedding. Probably the only two lesbians within 100 Miles so clearly we would get along."

"Naturally," she said with a wink.

I cleared my throat to try to stop myself from salivating over that wink, then reached out my hand. "I'm Rory Montgomery, cousin of the bride. And you are?"

My soon-to-be-not-so-mystery girl took my hand. "I'm Jenny Hanson. Cousin of the groom."

I picked my drink up off of the bar and tapped it against her wine glass. "John never mentioned that he had such a beautiful cousin."

"John and I don't see each other much. My family lives in California."

"Oh yeah? What part? My dad moved to LA a few years ago, so I've visited a few times."

"Wrightwood. It's a small town about an hour and a half outside of LA. I'm actually in the process of trying to move closer to LA though. The small town life isn't for me."

I held up my hand for a high five. "Preach it sister. Me either."

Jenny raised an eyebrow at me. "So I take it you're from around here?"

I spread out my arms and took a look around.

"Cowtown. Born and raised. But I escaped. I'm living about 2 hours away in a suburb of Philadelphia. I highly suggest it. Escaping that is."

"I'll keep that in mind."

I wasn't ready for the conversation to end so I thought quickly. "And why don't you have a date? I would think traveling all the way from California would make you worthy of one."

Jenny raised her wine glass to her lips and took a teasingly slow sip. "I don't date," she said stiffly.

"Oh yeah? Celibate? Waiting for a princess to sweep you off your feet?"

Jenny slowly shook her head. "Not quite."

I decided to pry further. For some reason, I was desperate to figure out what this girl's deal was. "So. You completely don't date or you just don't bring dates to weddings?" I hesitated before adding, "I got it. You're saving yourself for marriage and bringing a date to a wedding would just be way too tempting."

Jenny leaned in close enough to whisper in my ear. "Quite the opposite actually," she revealed.

I felt my whole body heat up at this revelation, but willed my face to not turn red. Instead, I did my best mock gasp and threw a hand over my heart. "Miss Hanson. Your cousin must be so disappointed with you."

Jenny looked in the direction of John. "Like I said, we're not very close. I love my cousin, but there are certain things he doesn't need to know about me."

I felt a sly grin cross my face. "What? Like the fact that you..."

Jenny put a finger to my lips before I could finish my sentence. "Hey now. Let's not make any snap judgments. Just because I said I'm not waiting until marriage doesn't mean I'm getting into bed with a different girl every night. Let's just say I enjoy a little fun."

"And if that fun lasts until morning, you make sure you're out of there before the bacon and eggs start cooking." I threw a wink in for good measure.

"It looks like you've got me all figured out. I hope you won't judge me too much Miss Montgomery," Jenny quipped before finishing off the rest of her wine.

I shook my head. "Of course not. I also enjoy a good time. I just prefer to take a girl to dinner first."

Jenny sighed as she looked around the room. "This wedding could really use a pick me up. It's barely 7:00 and I feel like people are already considering going to bed."

I sat my empty drink on the bar, suddenly aware of my prior mission, then turned back to Jenny. "Don't worry.

I'm on it. I don't know what you've heard, but I'm kind of a good time."

Jenny shot me a questioning look. "Is that so? See the thing is, I've been told that I'm a great time. Getting the party going at weddings is kinda my thing."

I shook my head, laughing at the irony of the situation. "Are you messing with me now? I didn't know that could be someone's thing. At least not anyone else's thing, because it's actually mine."

I raised both eyebrows at Jenny in a sort of silent challenge.

The smile never left Jenny's face as she took one finger and tapped it against her lips as if she was contemplating my words.

After a few seconds, she stopped the tapping and stood up a little straighter. "Ok the way I see it, we have two options," she said seriously. "We can fight over who is the more fun one here. We will most likely spend the whole night in this feud and you will be sorely disappointed once you find out it's me. The second, better option would be to forget about competing and work together. God knows this wedding could use it."

Oh yeah. I definitely liked this girl. "I'm in. Just try not to let the fact that I literally am the party keep you from doing your part of the job."

Jenny shook her head and smiled widely at me. "Ok. Since you're so terrific, what's the plan?"

A smiled back at her, ready to accept her unspoken challenge. "Easy. Conga line."

Jenny sarcastically choked on a cough while rolling her eyes. "Really? You say you're some kind of pro and then suggest the oldest trick in the book?"

"Ok then. If you're so smart, give me your plan."

A mischievous grin spread across Jenny's face. "I see your conga line, but I raise you at least two choruses of 'shout' before we start it. If we are going cliche wedding, we're diving in all the way."

I rubbed my fingers across my chin in mock thought. "I like the way you think. Here's the plan. We grab as many people as we can out onto the dance floor for 'shout' and dance through the softer part and back into the louder part. Once everyone is jumping up and down, we form the conga line. You go in front of me and grab your cousin to go in front of you. I'll make my cousin join behind me. People will be excited to latch on to either the bride or groom. Deal?"

Jenny reached her hand out to me, like we were in the middle of a high stakes Las Vegas bet. "Deal. Let's get this party started."

I ran over to the DJ booth while Jenny made her way onto the dance floor. The DJ took my request and immediately switched on the song. As soon as it started, I began grabbing older relatives while Jenny made her way over to the high school boys. It didn't take us long to have a group of people out on the dance floor with us. By the time the climax of the song hit, everyone was jumping up and down. At that moment, I nodded at Jenny then put my hands on her hips, just above her butt. I knew exactly what I was doing when I came up with this plan and I was going to take full advantage of the opportunity to get my hands on those curves. I only removed one of my hands for a few seconds in order to grab my cousin as Jenny grabbed hers.

Soon, almost every person attending the wedding had joined the conga line and, much to my surprise, it lasted through two more songs. When it ended, everyone was out of breath and the DJ took that opportunity to turn on a slow song.

I turned to Jenny and reached out my hand. "Would you do me the honor, Miss Hanson?"

Jenny accepted my hand and curtsied. "It would be my pleasure," she said with a grin.

As we danced close together, I noticed that her hair smelled like vanilla and her body like cocoa butter, emitting the perfect combination.

"So, tell me something about yourself that I don't already know," I inquired.

"You don't know anything about me."

"Then this should be easy."

Jenny seemed to be deep in thought for a few seconds then remarked, "I graduated from UCLA 2 years ago with a bachelor of the arts degree in film and television."

I nodded my head nonchalantly, trying not to show just how cool I thought this girl was. "That's awesome. And what are you doing with that degree now?"

She sighed loudly and closed her eyes in embarrassment. "I'm doing what everyone with a film degree in California does. I'm waiting tables and bartending. Not so awesome anymore, I know. The tips aren't bad though."

"Hey everyone has to start somewhere," I reassured her. "What part of film are you interested in?"

Jenny looked up at the ceiling as if she was deep in thought. "I either want to do screenplay writing or producing. I love all the little pieces that go into making a film, all the behind the scenes details that no one thinks about."

I could see Jenny's face lighting up the more she talked about it and said a silent prayer that she would be able to find a job she loved soon. "I'm sure something will come along. You just have to be patient."

"I did get an offer from a small independent film company I did an internship with in college. I just haven't decided if I'm going to take it yet," she admitted.

I raised an eyebrow at her. "Why wouldn't you take it? Not into small companies? Looking to be under the shining lights with Hollywood's greatest?"

Jenny shook her head forcefully. "Not at all. I actually have no interest in that. Working for an independent company would be a dream come true. It's all of the joys of film making without any of the spotlight BS. It's just that the position is the lowest of the low. It's pretty much just a paid internship and I don't even know if I'll make enough money to cover bills and rent. My parents offered to help, but I hate depending on them. The one positive is that there is a good chance I could move up in the company fairly quickly." She sighed loudly before continuing. "I just don't know if I'm chasing a pipe dream. Part of me thinks I should just let go and live in the real world. I have a writing minor. It wouldn't be too hard for me to go back to school and take some teaching classes so I could be an English teacher. It's not my dream but it's stable."

At this point, the slow song had ended, but I continued to hold onto Jenny. I looked deep into her eyes as I spoke. "You should do it. I know I just met you and it's none of my business, but I can see the way you light up when you talk about it. I think it's worth going for it. You're only 24. You don't have to enter the real world yet. Plus, who's to say this isn't the real world for you?"

Jenny nodded her head in understanding. "You make a good point. Apparently you're not just eye candy Rory Montgomery." She winked before adding, "But here I am being so rude. I haven't even asked about what you do."

Before answering, I took a moment to look around the room and noticed that even though the DJ had switched back to a fast song, it looked like people were starting to stare longingly at their seats. As much as I wanted to spend the night talking to Jenny, I knew I owed it to my cousin to make sure her wedding was a success.

"I would love to bore you with all of those details, but for now, we have a job to do," I informed Jenny. "You take the high school boys. Flirt with them a bit to keep them on the dance floor. If you keep them out there, the girls will stay too. I'll take the older crowd. I'll charm them into dancing with me."

I followed my instructions with a wide grin, hoping she didn't mind that I had just put her on hormonal boy duty. If she did, she didn't show it. She bumped her hip against mine then made her way toward the group of teenage boys congregating at the edge of the dance floor. As she walked, she made sure to sway her body back and forth. When she reached the group, she gently placed her hand on the one boy's shoulder, then whispered something in his ear. She followed up this action by turning around and winking at me. My God. How many hours were left in this wedding? This girl was going to be the death of me.

I tried to shake myself of the thoughts that would make me the equivalent of a teenage boy myself and made my way over to my grandma who seemed to be walking toward her table with the other older members of our family. Before she could sit down, I grabbed her arm.

"Hey hey young lady," I scolded. "Just where do you think you're going? I haven't gotten my dance yet."

My grandma waved her hand in my direction in an effort to shush me, but she should have known I wouldn't give up that easily. I moved my hand over my face as if I was wiping tears away.

"Aw come on grandma Helen. You're going to break my heart. Is that really what you want to do to your FAVORITE grandchild?"

My grandma shook her head at me, but I could see a smile starting to spread across her face. "You know I don't have favorites. But I must remind you that I am your favorite grandma and if you make me dance much longer, you might kill me."

She was right about that. She was my favorite grandma. Although, she never really had any competition. I had never had much of a relationship with my grandparents on my dad's side. His father passed away when I was only 5 and his mother passed away when I was 12, but I had only met her a handful of times. She lived in Florida and didn't really make time for her family. Like mother, like son I guess.

"You might be my favorite grandma, but that doesn't mean you're automatically my favorite grandparent. Grandpa could still beat you out at that and I bet he will dance with me if I ask him. Isn't that right gramps?"

At this my grandpa looked up from his seat, where he was almost falling asleep and muttered a quick, "Oh yeah sure. Whatever you say sweetheart."

I turned to grandma Helen with a victorious smile. "See. Told you," I said while raising my eyebrows at her.

She rolled her eyes then took my hand. "Fine. Let's get this over with." She paused and looked back at her white haired posse behind her. "Come on ladies and gents. We have to put on our dancing shoes for just a few more songs for my granddaughter."

Soon I was out on the dance floor, twisting and turning with everyone over the age of 70 at the wedding. Time passed by quickly and I was happy that I had been successful at keeping the older generation on the dance floor for a decent amount of songs and that they seemed to have forgotten about wanting to sit. As often as I could, I turned to look at Jenny on the dance floor. Now and then, she would look over at the same time and smile at me in a way that made butterflies flutter through my stomach. Man, what was wrong with me.

After a few more songs, my cousin joined my grandma and I. She leaned in close and whispered just loud enough for me to make out what she was saying.

"You're off wedding hype duty. You did a good job. Now go dance with John's cousin. You've only been staring at her *all night.*"

"Have not," I tried to argue, but the blush on my face told her otherwise.

Valerie threw back her head in laughter. "Ok. Whatever you say Ror. Would you stop arguing with me and just go dance with her?"

"Fine," I said. "But only because you told me to and it's your day."

She smiled at me knowingly as I scurried away. I found Jenny patting the head of a boy from Valerie's graduating class. "I told you dude. Even if you were five years older, you still wouldn't be my type."

Just as she finished her sentence she caught me standing beside her and a wide grin spread across her face. She pointed to me. "Now if you looked more like this one right here, you would totally be my type."

A look of confusion entered onto the boy's face as he looked between Jenny and I, but suddenly his face became like a kid on Christmas when it clicked that Jenny and I were lesbians.

He threw an arm around each of us. "So ladies, how would you feel about…"

I put a hand over his mouth before he could complete his thought and moved an elbow toward his junk, stopping myself right before I hit the target. "Finish that sentence and you'll find out how it feels to lose the ability to ever be able to make babies."

His eyes went wide as he quickly backed away from us. He put both hands in the air in a sign of surrender. "So sorry ladies. You two do whatever it is you want to do. Forget about me. So sorry."

He tripped over his own feet and stumbled into a

group of girls and guys his age. Jenny and I looked at each other and both broke into laughter at the same time.

Jenny shook her head. "Boys. What to do with them?"

I reached my hand out toward her. "I can think of a good amount of things NOT to do with them. And one of those things is dance. That, I would rather do with you."

"You think you're such a smooth talker, don't you Miss Montgomery?" Jenny lifted an eyebrow at me, but proceeded to take my hand.

We spent the rest of the wedding dancing with each other and made sure to keep it *mostly* pg. As the last song played, Jenny leaned in close to whisper in my ear.

"You know, this is normally the point in the night when I would kiss you and ask you if you wanted to come back to my room, but I'm not going to do that."

A mixture of excitement and disappointment shot through me. It felt good that this gorgeous girl was clearly enjoying my company just as much as I was enjoying hers, but clearly it wasn't enough to keep the night from ending.

I leaned in close to whisper back to her. "Oh yeah? And why is that?"

At this, Jenny grabbed my hand and dragged me toward the exit of the reception hall. The cool October air sent a shiver down my spine as we sat down on a bench a few yards from the hall. Although I wasn't sure if it was definitely the air or the girl sitting next to me that was causing the chill.

Jenny kept her hand on mine as she started to speak. "I like you Rory."

Before I could control it, I felt a goofy grin take over my face. Jenny must have noticed it too because she rolled her eyes at me.

"Whoa, calm down killer. Not like that. You can put the breaks on planning our wedding."

I let out a disgusted moan. "I would never! I don't plan to date someone for more than three months, let alone marry them."

And it was true. As much as I had grown to like Jenny over the past few hours, she wasn't going to be the girl to suddenly change me. I decided from a young age that long term relationships just weren't for me and even the most gorgeous girl I'd ever laid eyes on couldn't change that.

Jenny giggled and I couldn't help but notice how she batted her eyelashes while she did.

"As I was saying," she continued, "I like you. You're one of the most down to earth people I have ever met. Not to mention, you're not so bad to look at either. That is exactly why nothing can happen between us. I think we could be good friends and a random hookup would ruin that. Plus, you would want to take me to dinner and text me lovey things for three months before cutting me off completely and none of that sounds like fun to me."

I stuck my hand out to Jenny, motioning for her to shake it. "Deal. Friends it is. I like the way you think. I'm happy one of us is capable of thinking with their brain and not, well, something else. But as your friend, could I ask for your number? I want updates on this job of yours."

Without saying anything, Jenny reached for my purse and grabbed my phone out. She hit a few buttons then handed it back to me. I looked down to see a text message reading *hey there cutie* sent to the contact "Wedding Jenny."

I raised an eyebrow at her. "Wedding Jenny, huh?"

She lifted her shoulders slightly. "Hey, who knows how many girls named Jenny you talk to. Had to make it something you would remember."

"Again. So smart," I remarked. "By the way, is this text your way of telling me that you think I'm cute?"

Jenny gave me a half smile. "That text was sent from *your* phone so technically you think I'm cute."

I laughed and shook my head. "Well, I'm not going to disagree with that. You're one of a kind wedding Jenny."

Jenny squeezed my hand then stood up. "I better be heading to bed. We're flying back to California early tomorrow morning." She hesitated then added, "Would it be ok if I asked you for a friendly hug?"

I nodded and stood up. As Jenny wrapped her arms around me, I held her close taking in her scent, not knowing if I would ever see her again, but secretly wishing that I would.

Chapter 2

"Hey lovely. How would you feel about me taking you to dinner tonight?" I finished the text and looked back at my laptop, forcing myself to focus. I had a ton of emails to answer and meetings to set up if I wanted to actually have time for said dinner.

I answered a few of the emails, then looked back at my phone to see a text message come in from Jenny.

"Hey there. Do you have any free time to chat today? I have an update on the LA situation that I want to share with you."

Before I had the chance to answer Jenny, I received a reply from Morgan, or as Jenny liked to call her - my flavor of the week. "Dinner sounds wonderful. Where were you thinking?"

I told her it was her choice, then brought the phone up to my ear to call Jenny. It had been 4 months since we met at my cousin's wedding and we had grown surprisingly close in that time, texting or calling each other almost every day. She picked up after just a few rings and giggled into the phone.

"Well, that was quick. You must miss me."

"You know I do, plus I'm dying to hear the update you have for me."

Jenny had been keeping me updated with her job offer in LA. Soon after the wedding she agreed to take the job, but the position wasn't available until January. She was having trouble finding housing she could afford in the area so for the past month she had been working there 2-3 long days a week and commuting. Her boss had been understanding of it, but during our last call she told me that she thought his patience was running thin.

"I have good news," Jenny announced. "Stalking Craigslist finally worked. A guy who is just two years older than us posted an ad that he is looking for someone to split the rent in his apartment. It's a small one bedroom so it's definitely not super convenient, but it's the lowest I would ever pay in LA. The best part is that it's within a mile of work so I can just walk there."

I was happy that Jenny and I hadn't decided to FaceTime for this call because I didn't want her to see the skeptical look on my face. "That sounds great," I lied.

"You don't have to lie to me, you know. My family looked at me like I was crazy when I told them about it."

"I just have a few questions, like how this living arrangement is going to work and how I can be sure that this guy isn't going to murder you," I questioned.

Jenny laughed again. "The living arrangement isn't so

fun. It's literally going to be like college. Two twin size beds in a shared room with shared closet space. And about the whole murder thing - I *have* done my research. He friended me on Facebook, sent me a link to his nonprofit that has his picture on the website, and we Skyped this morning. It all checks out. I'm actually driving to LA now to meet him. If it goes ok and isn't super awkward, I'm just going to sleep on the couch tonight so I don't have to drive back for work tomorrow."

I felt a ball form in the pit of my stomach. It sounded like Jenny had done her research, but I still worried about her. "Could you at least send me his address?" I asked, then added, "I'd also feel better if you met him somewhere in public to start."

I could almost feel Jenny rolling her eyes at me through the phone. "You sound like my parents, but I'll send you the address of his apartment AND the address of where I am meeting him, which is the Unicorn Cove - a very public place that happens to be the non profit that he owns. It's a safe space for lgbt kids to go hang out and feel like they fit in. They also provide counselors for those struggling. And before you ask, yes he is gay."

"You're definitely getting murdered," I proclaimed. "Someone this great doesn't actually exist."

"If I do get murdered, at least I can be content knowing that I already met the prettiest girl in the world. But I better focus on this drive. Traffic is picking up. I'll send you the addresses once I'm out of the car, but for now you can look up Unicorn Cove."

"Sounds good. I should be getting back to work anyway," I said with a sigh.

"Oh you mean this super secret job of yours that you refuse to tell me anything about?"

I shook my head at Jenny. It's not that I was trying to keep my job a secret from her. I just didn't feel the need to talk about it all the time. "I've told you. It's not a secret. I just don't want to bore you with the details."

"Ok whatever," Jenny quipped. "I'll talk to you later. Have a good night Miss Montgomery."

"You too Wedding Jenny. Bye."

When I hung up the phone, I noticed a huge grin had spread across my face which seemed to be the norm whenever I talked to Jenny. I quickly typed Unicorn Cove into the search on my computer and did a sweep of the site to make sure it seemed legit. Once I decided it passed, I looked back at my phone to check my text from Morgan, who had suggested an Italian restaurant about a half hour from me.

I looked at the clock which now read 3:30 and told

her that I would pick her up at 6:30. This would give me another hour to do work and then an hour and a half to get ready. Morgan was a nice girl. She was a second grade teacher and deserved a little effort. I had been on a few dates with her over the past month, some that lasted all night.

A few minutes before 6:30, I was pulling up outside of Morgan's apartment building. I parked and hit the button for her apartment number so she could buzz me in. When I walked in, I found Morgan putting on her shoes which were gold high heels. Her curly blonde hair was resting on her tan shoulders and she was wearing a green sundress. Seeing her in green made my mind immediately flash to Jenny and how good she looked at the wedding. That look was ingrained in me since it was the first time we met, but I have to say that all of the times I have seen her since through FaceTime and Skype have been just as good. I had to shake these thoughts from my head though. I was on a date with Morgan. Jenny was my friend and that's all she would ever be. It made sense that way. Why risk our friendship over a relationship that was doomed from the beginning? Neither of us had any plans on staying in any sort of lasting romantic relationship and that wasn't going to change.

I was surprised to feel a pair of lips on my cheek. I had been so caught up in my thoughts that I hadn't realized that Morgan had stood up and made her way over to me and was now standing beside me.

Ready?" I asked while flashing her a thousand watt smile.

If she had caught on to the fact that I had completely zoned out from the world around me, she didn't let onto it as she took my arm that I had offered her.

When we arrived at the restaurant, we made small talk about work and what her class was learning now. One thing I liked about Morgan was how much she lit up when she talked about teaching. It wasn't as much as Jenny had lit up when she talked about filmmaking but... damn it... why was my mind going back to Jenny again? It must have just been the worry over her trip to LA. I felt like my phone was burning a hole in my purse, but I refused to take it out to check if I had any messages from her. I wasn't going to ignore my date to focus on my phone.

By the time we were waiting for dessert, my anxiety over Jenny had gotten the best of me so I excused myself to the bathroom so I could check my phone. As soon as I was in a stall, I took it out and looked through the messages she had sent me. She had sent me a few updates with addresses and how things were going.

The final message had come through about 10

minutes ago and was a picture of her and the guy, whose name I now knew was Ryan from stalking his non profit website, and a caption that read "Look! It's really him (and he doesn't have an ax)!"

Out of a gut reaction, I immediately went into Jenny's contact information and started a FaceTime call to her. Much to my relief, she picked up after only two rings. Only it wasn't just her staring at me through the screen. Ryan was standing right there beside her. Both he and Jenny had big smiles on their faces.

Ryan was the one to start speaking first. "I feel like I should just introduce myself since I hear you are very worried about my intentions with your friend. But first, I gotta say that I'm flattered. It's been a long time since anyone has worried about my intentions with a girl. I'm Ryan Wright by the way. And before you say anything, I'm not sure why my parents thought that was a good name either. If you want to hear something really embarrassing, my middle name is actually Roy."

He rolled his eyes then stuck out his tongue. I had to laugh. I liked this guy and was already feeling a thousand times better about Jenny being with him.

I noticed Jenny giving me strange look as she tried to take in my surroundings. "Are you in a bathroom stall right now? You totally are. Why are you FaceTiming us from a bathroom stall?"

I hesitated, then tried my best to put on an innocent grin. "I'm kind of… on a date right now."

As soon as the words left my mouth, both Ryan and Jenny started to laugh. Jenny shook her head at me. "My oh my. You certainly are one of a kind. You should probably go though. I know I'm not up on the dating game, but I don't believe girls like it when you sneak away from your date to FaceTime with a girl that you find to be devastatingly gorgeous."

Ryan nodded in agreement and I couldn't help but think about how much my best friend Todd would like him. I know, it's super stereotypical and such a heterosexual thing to do to think that every gay person would get along. But something told me that they would.

I said my goodbyes then slipped out of the bathroom. When I got back to the table, I noticed that our dessert, a cheesecake that we had decided to split, had already arrived.

Morgan gave me a concerned look. "Are you feeling ok? You were gone awhile."

"Yeah, sorry. I had a few text messages I had to answer from a friend. She was meeting someone off of Craigslist tonight, so I was a bit worried and noticed I had some texts from her when I checked my phone quickly. I'm really sorry." I never understood the point in lying. I saw no reason for it. Plus, the truth was better than the alternative that would have kept me in the bathroom so long.

Morgan smiled at me as she took a bite of cheesecake. I felt much more relaxed the rest of our time together since I knew everything was alright with Jenny.

After finding a parking spot at her apartment, I made sure to hurry around to open Morgan's car door for her then escorted her to the door of her apartment. After I kissed her goodnight, she flashed me a suggestive smile.

"You can come in if you want," she suggested.

Normally, I would jump at this offer, but for whatever reason, I wasn't in the mood tonight. "I think I'm just going to sleep in my own bed tonight if that's ok. I'm really tired."

Even as the words came out of my mouth, I couldn't believe I was saying them.

Morgan looked concerned. "Are you sure you're ok?"

I sighed, louder than I had intended to. Morgan was such a nice girl. She was pretty, funny, and super chill. I often wondered what was wrong with me that I didn't want a lasting relationship when I had a girl like this right in front of me. Well, actually I knew exactly what was wrong with me, but it wasn't worth thinking about right now.

Morgan must have noticed the distant look in my eyes because she took my hand and smiled at me. "Is this the point where you tell me that things are done between us? That this little fling has run it's course? Because you can just say it Rory. I'm a big girl. I knew what the deal was when we started hanging out. You're a very honest person and I really like that about you."

I sighed again. "I don't know Morgan. I'm going to be traveling a lot over the next two weeks and I don't want to make any guarantees. I also don't want to hold you back from anything."

Morgan squeezed my hand. "Hey. Don't worry about it. You have nothing to feel bad about. If I'm being completely honest, I'm not completely over my ex yet. But you've been a big help at keeping me distracted over this past month. And, hey, if you get back and want to hang out again, just give me a call. But don't worry, I won't sit by the phone waiting for it."

I was relieved to hear what Morgan had to say. It wasn't surprising that she wasn't over her ex. She had just gotten out of a three year relationship four months ago. The truth was, I liked dating girls who were on the rebound. Most people who dated on the rebound weren't expecting it to last. I had actually dated a lot of girls who ended up getting back together with their ex after dating me. And I was fine with that. I liked being the girl who helped someone realize they still loved their ex or even that they deserved much better than their ex.

I gave Morgan one last kiss and squeezed her hand. "You're a really good person. I hope everything works out for you." I hesitated, then added, "By the way, feel free to get ahold of me whenever you want. Don't hesitate to call if you need anything, ever. I'm here for you. I mean it."

Morgan smiled. "I know you do and I appreciate that. Goodbye Rory."

I said goodbye to Morgan and even though I tried to tell myself it wasn't definitely the last time I would be seeing her, I had a feeling it was. Once I was in my car, I decided to give Jenny another call. It seemed crazy to be calling her for the third time in one day, but I just wanted to check up on her one last time before I went to bed.

The phone rang through my bluetooth many times and I figured it was going to go to voicemail, but Jenny picked up on what I assumed had to be the last ring. "Ditching your date to call me again?"

I smiled at the speakers in my car like an idiot. "Just wanted to check up on you one more time and make sure you're ok."

I heard Ryan shout something in the background and Jenny laughed. "Ryan says you called too early. The murdering isn't happening for a few hours."

"Well, at least I was able to hear your voice one more time before it happens," I said sarcastically.

Jenny's voice became serious. "But honestly, shouldn't you still be on your date? Until like...I don't know..tomorrow?"

"I decided to end things early tonight," I admitted.

"So, is the Morgan fling over now? On to the next one?" Jenny questioned.

"I'm not sure. We kind of left it open ended." Even as the words left my mouth, I didn't really believe them.

"Open ended, huh? You'll have to let me know what happens," Jenny joked. Then she hesitated for a moment and her voice took on a more serious tone. "Actually, I've been thinking. I'm sure you would agree that you and I have a pretty flirtatious friendship. And even though the flirtation obviously doesn't mean anything to either of us, I feel like it takes some of the fun away when we talk about our dates and hookups. Maybe we could agree to not discuss that part of our lives with each other."

I thought about Jenny's proposition. I liked it and was actually disappointed that I hadn't been the one to suggest it.

For whatever reason, I hated hearing about Jenny's nights out and her hookups. I'm not sure why. I didn't mind hearing about any of my other friends' sexcapades and that's all Jenny and I were - friends. So what if our friendship had started out with me hoping she would invite me back to her hotel room? Or that I still found her to be the most beautiful girl in the world? None of that should have mattered. But no matter what the reasoning was, I liked this new arrangement.

"I'm in," I said cheerfully. "No more girl talk."

"Unless it involves the two pretty girls who are having the conversation," Jenny added and I could just imagine the flirtatious smile on her face.

I heard Ryan shout something else in the background. "Mind sharing the comments from the peanut gallery?" I asked.

Jenny laughed. "He just seems to think the two of us and this friendship of ours is super strange. I disagree obviously. I think it's great."

I scoffed. "Tell him he can keep those opinions to himself when you guys move in together. I happen to like our friendship."

And I did like my friendship with Jenny. I really really liked it.

Chapter 3

I rolled over in my hotel room bed and checked the time on the clock. For a minute I couldn't even remember what time zone I was in let alone what city. Sometimes I felt like I traveled more than I was home. Most of that was my own choice though. Yes, I had to in order to earn a living, but I also loved it. When I looked out my window and saw the Las Vegas strip, I was reminded where I was and why I had just slept until almost 1pm. It had been a fun night the night before, hanging out with a group of girls that I had met at the club and not rolling into my room until around 4am.

I turned on my computer to check my email and noticed that I had one with a subject that piqued my interest. "Request for a favor" was the title and normally I would have figured this was just junk, but the email address contained the first and last name (Jeremiah Hall) of a guy I had graduated with. I say a guy I graduated with because I wouldn't exactly call him a friend. Not that there was anything wrong with him. We just didn't run with the same crowds, to say the least. He was the president of the Future Farmers of America, while I was secretly wishing that our school would somehow decide to form a gay straight alliance.

I opened the email and began to read.

Hey Rory. I know it's been forever since we talked. I actually saw you from afar at your cousin's wedding, but since you were with your family and girlfriend, I didn't want to bother you. I have a strange favor to ask you. I just proposed to Samantha last week and we are planning a wedding for the middle of June. I know it's really soon, but we just wanted to get it done quickly and keep it on the cheaper end. I was wondering if you had any interest in being somewhat of a stand in DJ. My friend is going to provide the speakers and a microphone and we are just going to attach an ipod to the speakers as well. I'm going to add music so it's just a matter of deciding what is best to play when and announcing things such as the wedding party, dinner, and dances. I know this isn't what you do, but you really were the reason that John and Valerie's wedding was so much fun. Unfortunately, I can't pay you, but I can provide you with a free meal and drinks and you're welcome to bring your girlfriend along to the wedding with you. My phone number is listed below. Just send me a text and let me know what you think. It's ok if you don't want to. I just thought I would ask. But if you could text me and let me know either way, it would be really appreciated. Thanks Rory and congrats on all your success the past few years. I hope life is treating you as well as it seems to be.

As I finished the email, a few things stuck out to me. First of all, I had to believe that the rumors I had heard were true. Just last week my mom called to tell me that the ladies in her book club were buzzing about how one of the guys I graduated with had gotten his girlfriend pregnant...out of wedlock (gasp) and it was Farmer Ted's son to boot. My mom wasn't a fan of the small town gossip, but she always shared it with me because we got a good laugh out of it. I made a mental note to tell her about Jeremiah's shotgun wedding that pointed to a pregnant soon-to-be wife. I was also surprised to see that Jeremiah was still so cool with me since I had come out. Sure, I had been out since high school and no one ever said too much about it (honestly most of the small minded people in my town just tried to pretend it wasn't true), but Jeremiah didn't strike me as a guy who would be ok with homosexuality. Then again, that was me being super judgmental. Just because someone was a redneck born and raised didn't mean they couldn't be open minded.

The part of the email that confused me was how Jeremiah kept referring to my girlfriend. I dated a lot of girls, but none from our town and I certainly didn't have anyone at the wedding with me. I decided just to text him so I could clear up any confusion there might be.

"Hey Jeremiah," I wrote. "I would be happy to get the

party going at your wedding. Incase you didn't know, it's one of my favorite things. But just so you know, I don't have a girlfriend."

Within seconds I had a reply. "Wow. That's amazing. Thank you so much. We can talk about details later, but if you have any questions in the meantime, feel free to call or text."

Before I could reply, another text came through from him. "By the way...I'm sorry I brought up the girlfriend thing. I didn't realize you two had broken up. I have to admit, I'm a bit disappointed. She was a hoot at your cousin's wedding. I was hoping to have you both."

My confusion was at an all time high as he sent another text. "Sorry. I shouldn't have said all of that. It was really insensitive of me. I'm sure it hasn't been easy for you..."

I broke into laughter as it finally hit me who he was talking about and I typed a text back to him. "HA! Jeremiah, you don't happen to be talking about the brown haired, shimmery eyed bombshell in the green dress, do you?"

"Yes..." was the only response I received.

I laughed more as I typed out my reply. "Dude. Nothing to feel bad about. That was John's cousin, not my girlfriend. I hadn't even met her before that night at the wedding. She's from California."

Jeremiah sent back an emoji that had an embarrassed look and red cheeks. "I'm so sorry. I just assumed she was your girlfriend since I saw you guys together most of the night. I shouldn't have made that assumption though. My bad. If I haven't stuck my foot in my mouth too much and you're still willing to do this, you are welcome to bring anyone you'd like with you. Obviously, I wouldn't complain about that bombshell (as you so nicely put it) from Cali flying in, but since you probably haven't talked to her since that night, feel free to invite whoever."

I sent him one more text telling him that I was definitely still willing to play DJ Rory for the night and I would let him know who I decided to bring. I immediately called Jenny, hoping I could catch her on her lunch break since we were actually in the same time zone for once.

"Hey there pretty girl," she said after a few rings. "I only have about 15 minutes of my lunch break left, but I'm totally willing to spend those last precious minutes chatting with my favorite gal."

I tried to ignore how warm my body felt when she said things like that. It was ridiculous for me to have that sort of reaction.

"No worries," I said once I found my voice. "I just

have a funny story to tell you."

I told her all about my email from Jeremiah and how he had requested for her to come along with me. I left out the part about him mistakenly calling her my girlfriend because, for some reason, it felt strange to bring up to her.

By the time I finished the story, we were both laughing. "Wow. We left quite the impression, didn't we? I'm just not sure why he emailed you instead of me. I was clearly the better time that night. It must have to do with proximity and your history."

"Oh yes. That must be it. It couldn't have anything to do with the fact that I AM the party," I said sarcastically.

"It's too bad though," Jenny remarked. "If I didn't live so far away and you *actually* invited me, I would totally go with you."

"Well, consider this my official invitation. If you are willing to travel to Pennsylvania, I would love for you to come play DJ with me." I held my breath, wondering what her answer would be.

"I would actually love to do that," Jenny said, but her disappointed tone told me there was a but coming. "But you know I can't afford to fly across the country just to spend the weekend at a wedding. Between my low paying job and the cost of living in LA, that's just not in my budget right now."

"I could…" I paused for a moment wondering if I should continue my thought. "Get your ticket for you. I have enough frequent flyer miles because of traveling for work."

"But don't you actually use those frequent flyer miles for your work trips?" Jenny asked. "You would end up paying for it in the future."

I sighed. "Listen. I've never been totally transparent with you about my job and financial situation, but money isn't really an issue for me and I would really like it if you would come. Anything I have to pay would be worth it for the good time we would have."

Jenny was silent for what felt like forever. "Send me the details and I'll think about it. I can't talk now, but I'll call you after work if it's not too late for you."

"I'm in Vegas so it definitely won't be too late." When Jenny didn't respond, I added, "I'm in Vegas for work related purposes. Just so you know. This isn't in our 'cannot speak about' clause"

Jenny laughed and it sounded like some tension was washing away. But why should she feel tense about me being in Las Vegas for personal reasons? It was probably just my imagination. We said goodbye and she promised to call me on her way home from work.

A few hours and a few meetings later, just as

promised, my phone rang.

"Hello there," I answered cheerfully.

"Ok spill," Jenny said in her best fake stern voice. "What is this big, fancy, high paying job you decided to keep a secret from me for some reason? And who is your boss? Want to give him my resume?"

"Funny you should say that," I remarked. "You're actually talking to my boss right now. I kind of run my own thing."

"Care to elaborate what this 'thing' is?"

I went on to explain the whole story to her. It all started in my last year of college when we had to make and advertise a new product. Instead of making an actual product, I decided to make up a new social media platform. Since I had taken classes in coding and web design and was kind of an overachiever, I had gone ahead and actually gotten it up and running. It turned out that my professor really thought I was on to something and encouraged me to continue even after the project was over. It all kind of spiraled out from there. It was never going to be facebook or twitter, but the idea actually resonated with many people. I guess the fact that I grew up in a small town and then went to school in a big city was the inspiration behind it. I was able to see the good in both small businesses as well as corporations, so I developed a social media site that brought the two together. I created a form of social media that was for businesses. Small businesses can advertise their products and big businesses could pick up a product that they would never know about otherwise. For example, if a certain mom and pop shop had great grandma's old recipe for "to die for" brownies, they could advertise and sell that recipe to a large grocery store so they were able to make extra money in order to keep their business from shutting down. Pretty much it was a way for businesses to work together instead of competing.

Jenny was listening intently so I kept explaining how the businesses paid a monthly fee to join the social network and once they were on there they could post updates about their business, share information with other businesses, or put out advertisements. All my travel time was spent either pitching to businesses about why they should join or trying to get people to sponsor my endeavors. Sponsors would have their advertisements pop up randomly on a business feed that could benefit from their product (I used a complicated algorithm to make sure the sponsors showed up for the right people, using the same idea phone companies do to make sure your phone suddenly starts bringing up advertisements for cat food as soon as you mention the word cat to someone in the vicinity of your phone).

When I was finished with my explanation, Jenny was completely silent. I cleared my throat to try to gain her attention. "So did I put you to sleep?"

"No Rory," she said seriously. "I'm just at a loss for words. I'm not sure why you don't go around bragging about that to every person you know. I always figured you were smart, but...wow. You're amazing."

It was the most sincere I had ever heard Jenny sound. It wasn't to say that I didn't find her to be sincere, but most of her words had at least a hint of flirtation behind them. But this was different. This response had me feeling choked up for whatever reason. I tried to push those feelings down. I didn't want to show my vulnerability. I had no reason to feel vulnerable right now.

I took a deep breath and was finally able to regain my composure. "Well, since I'm so amazing, how would you feel about being DJ number 2 at this wedding with me?"

Jenny hesitated for only a moment before agreeing. "What the heck? I'm in. I probably shouldn't ask for more than one day off at this point though, so what if I take the first flight out to Philadelphia that Friday morning and I'll fly back later in the day on Sunday?"

"Sounds good to me," I answered cheerfully. "I'll start looking up flights."

As soon as we were off the phone, I started searching flights on my computer. I wondered what it would be like to see Jenny again. Would we have as much fun together at this wedding as we did at our cousins'? After having become friends over the past few months, would my stomach still go into knots at the sight of her?

Chapter 4

I stood at the bottom of the escalators holding a sign that I had made that read "Miss Jenny Hanson." I couldn't believe how fast the past two months had gone and the anxiety of seeing Jenny any minute was building inside of me. Anytime I caught a glimpse of brown hair, my heart started beating more rapidly. What was wrong with me? I didn't even get this nervous for dates, so why was I so nervous to pick a friend up from the airport?

Within a few minutes, it was Jenny coming down the escalator. Her brown hair was pulled up in a ponytail and she was wearing UCLA sweatpants and a white t-shirt, a big difference from her look at the wedding, but she somehow still looked just as gorgeous. As soon as she noticed me, I saw that right dimple form on her cheek as a smile spread across her face.

"Well aren't you a sight for sore eyes?" Jenny said as she dropped her carry on bags and wrapped her arms around me. Almost as soon as the hug had started, it was over and I found myself wishing it would last longer - for friendly reasons of course. Our whole friendship so far had been a series of telephone calls and video chats and it felt good to physically be in her presence.

I picked up her bags and led her out to my car. It was 2:00 and was going to take us about 2 hours to get back to my hometown. The plan was to drop Jenny off at her aunt and uncle's house, where she would be staying so she could get settled in. Then at 6:30, we had reservations at a little diner in town and by reservations I mean that we had practically rented out the whole restaurant since there were so many of us going. It was going to be the two of us, Jenny's aunt and uncle, her cousins John, Mary, and Paul, my aunt and uncle, my cousins Valerie and Pam, my mom, and my best friend Todd, who insisted on crashing our two family dinner so he could meet Jenny.

When I dropped her off, I found myself aching over the two hours that I would have to spend without her. Luckily, it flew by and soon I was in the car with my mom picking up Todd. Todd came out of his childhood home wearing khaki pants, a blue button up, and a rainbow bow tie. His short brown hair was just perfectly barely spiked. I shook my head at him as he climbed into the car. It was always like him to overdress and he currently had me feeling bad about the ripped black jeans and white t-shirt I was wearing.

"Don't give me that judgmental look," he lectured. "It's not my fault that you are fashionably inept compared to me."

I tried to sneak the middle finger at him without my mom, who was sitting in the passenger seat, noticing, but Todd wasn't going to let me get away with that.

He gasped and put his hand on his chest dramatically. "Mrs. Montgomery. Did you just see your daughter make an obscene gesture at me? Certainly that's not how a distinguished Montgomery woman should act."

Luckily, my mom just shook her head and laughed at us. She was used to our antics by now. Todd and I had been best friends since 7th grade when we discovered that we were both gay. We grew even closer when we decided to come out in high school, which surprisingly didn't go too bad given the small town we were from. Of course, there were some bible thumpers who tried to direct us toward Jesus and away from sin, but everyone else had been pretty open minded about it. I guess I should be honest though. It was much easier for me than it was for Todd. He had to endure some bullying in the locker room because high school guys are douchebags, but I quickly took him under my wing and into my tight knit friend group.

I heard a throat clear behind me and looked around to see my mom and Todd staring at me. I had been so caught up in my thoughts that I must have missed the conversation.

I smiled at them guiltily and shrugged my shoulders.

"Mind repeating that? I was just in my own little world."

Todd leaned forward between my mom and I. "I was just asking your mom about her thoughts on this *friendship* between you and Jenny."

He made air quotes as he said the word friendship.

I glared at him while I felt my face become red and then turned to my mom. "And what was your response?" I asked with a raised eyebrow.

My mom lifted both hands in surrender. "I told him that it's none of my business. You can be friends or more with whoever you want as long as they treat you well."

I smiled at my mom as Todd stuck his head between us again. "But we both totally agree that you want to be on the *more* side with Jenny."

"Obviously I don't," I fought back. "I mean look at how many girls I have dated since meeting Jenny at that wedding."

"You have dated three," Todd stated with a smug grin on his face. "Which is an average of one every two months and that's low for you, especially considering that you didn't date any of them for more than 3 weeks. That means that since the wedding, you have spent approximately 25 weeks single, which is pretty unthinkable for Rory Montgomery."

While I was impressed with his quick math, I was

annoyed at where he was putting his efforts in, especially since I was pretty sure he was exaggerating. I had dated Morgan for at least a month. The two girls who followed, Jessica and Alice, had been shorter than that, but I had also spent a lot of time traveling and I did mix some pleasure with fun on those business trips.

Luckily, our conversation was cut off when we pulled into the diner parking lot. We walked into the diner to find that a few booths had been reserved for us. Todd and I squeezed into the booth that already had the newlyweds (except after 8 months, I guess you couldn't call them that anymore) and Jenny in it, while my mom went to join her sister, brother in law, and my other two cousins.

I smiled over at Jenny as I took the seat beside her and tried to keep my eyes from lingering as I knew Todd was hanging on my every move. It was hard to tear my eyes away though. She looked so good wearing blue jeans and a red and gray baseball tee. Man, this girl could pull off any outfit.

I heard a throat clear beside me and realized that I had been caught. "Oh sorry. Todd, you know my cousin Valerie. This is her husband John, who I think you may have met at a family gathering in the past."

I took a breath and pointed my finger toward Jenny. "And this is Jenny - John's cousin."

"John's cousin," he repeated as a smirk spread across his face. Clearly, he found it amusing that I would introduce her this way.

I shot him a warning glance as he reached across me to shake her hand. "It's very nice to meet you Jenny. I've heard a lot about you. Surprisingly not from your cousin though. We don't really talk. You know, different grades and all of that. No, it's all from this girl. She talks about you so much, that I feel like I know you already."

Before I could respond to Todd's blatant disregard for the friendship code, I felt a hand squeeze my side. Jenny raised an eyebrow at me, then looked at Todd. "What can I say? This girl has good taste."

I squeezed my eyes shut, worried about how Todd would react to Jenny's flirtation.

"Let's talk about a more pressing matter," he said while squeezing my leg like he was trying to reassure me of something. "Tell me about this roommate of yours in LA. Is he single?"

We all laughed as I breathed a sigh of relief and Jenny told him all about Ryan, who was indeed single but unfortunately over 2,000 miles away.

The rest of the conversation flowed smoothly and luckily, Todd didn't say anything else to embarrass me. As the dinner came to an end and we all said our goodbyes, I felt sad that I had to say goodbye to Jenny again so soon. But luckily, we had already made plans for me to pick her up from her aunt and uncle's house early the next morning so we could have the whole day together leading up to the wedding.

The night seemed to drag on as I tossed and turned thinking about the next day with Jenny, again leaving me wondering what the heck was wrong with me. When my alarm went off at 8:00 the next morning, I felt like I had just barely shut my eyes but still forced myself to get up.

By 10:00, I was ringing the doorbell at Jenny's aunt and uncle's house. To my surprise, Jenny answered the door, with her shoes on and a bag with a change of clothes already packed.

As we walked to the car, I tried to sneak a peek into Jenny's bag to see what she was wearing for the wedding. The wedding attire was apparently "country casual" and when I asked Jeremiah what this meant, he had shrugged his shoulders and told me to wear whatever I wanted to.

Jenny had told me that she had the perfect outfit planned out, but wouldn't tell me what it was. Even now, she pulled her bag away as she caught my lingering eyes.

When we got back to my childhood home, I gave Jenny a tour. The house was filled with pictures, mostly of just my mom and I. There were a few with my grandma and grandpa and even fewer with my dad.

"It looks like you and your mom are really close," Jenny remarked as she ran her finger across a picture of her and I hugging at my preschool graduation.

"We are," I agreed. "She's like my best friend. We've been close forever, even before my dad left."

"When did he leave?" Jenny asked, with a hint of concern in her voice.

"Right after I left for college. They told me about the divorce that summer after I graduated." I lifted one shoulder and let it drop and tried my best to smile. "It wasn't a surprise to me. My parents just barely tolerated each other for as long as I could remember and my dad was never really home anyway. I know they only stayed together for me, but I'm not really sure how much difference it would have made if they had just ended it sooner. I think it probably just would have saved all of us years of heartache, but I do appreciate the thought behind it."

Jenny must have caught on to the fact that this wasn't something I really wanted to talk about because she squeezed my shoulder softly then asked to see my room.

I was embarrassed as I walked in and pictured myself as someone seeing this room for the first time. I hadn't changed the room at all since I was in high school - the walls were covered with movie posters and any open space had pictures cut out from magazines, mostly of female athletes. I found myself wishing I was showing Jenny my apartment instead. I was proud of the way I had decorated it. Clearly my taste had improved immensely in the past 6 years.

Jenny immediately started exploring the room and I cringed thinking about what she might find. She stood by my bookshelf for a long time, then reached down to pick something up. When she turned around to face me, I saw that she was holding my High School Musical box set.

Her smile was so wide, that her right dimple was even more pronounced than usual. "High School Musical fan, huh?"

I shrugged my shoulders. "You know how it is. I was young, in the closet, and liked to pretend that I had a crush on Zac Efron."

Jenny turned the box around and studied it. "Hm, that's funny that you should say that since it appears the last movie didn't come out until your freshman year in college, a whopping three years after the original came out. What year did you say you came out? Sophomore year of high school?"

I grabbed the dvds from her. "Ok. Whatever. You caught me. The music is really catchy and this movie is a

Disney Channel classic."

"I'm not saying I disagree with you," Jenny admitted.
"How would you feel about a little movie marathon?"

I quickly agreed. Where did this girl come from?
Gorgeous, caring, *and* willing to watch all three High School
Musical movies in one sitting? She really was the perfect
girl...you know...if you were the type of person that actually
believed in love stories and happily ever afters.

I put the first movie in and propped a few pillows up
on my bed. Sitting close to Jenny had the tendency to make
my mind wander. I thought about how much I wanted to
reach over and grab her hand or scoot closer to her and feel
her body up against mine. These were the type of things that
wouldn't even be a thought if I was with another girl. I would
have just done it. With Jenny, they were thoughts that I
shouldn't be having since we were just friends. Apparently,
Jenny didn't see it that way though because just a half hour
into the first movie, she wrapped her arm around mine and
laid her head on my shoulder. I felt my breath hitch with the
contact and had to remind myself to breathe. This must have
just been part of the package when you were "flirtatious
friends" as Jenny liked to call it. She was such a flirt that she
probably didn't even think anything of it.

Both times I had to get up to switch to the next DVD,

I worried that Jenny and I wouldn't return to our cuddling position, but both times as soon as I sat down, she wrapped herself around me again. As the third movie was coming to an end, I heard the front door open and my mom started walking up the stairs. I quickly jumped out of the bed, which was strange since it's not like I was doing anything wrong. Plus, I was a 24 year old adult who lived alone and had my own company. I wasn't some teenager sneaking a girl into my room in the middle of the night.

My mom knocked on my door, before letting herself in. When she walked into my room, she looked at the clock on the wall. "Shouldn't you guys be getting ready for the wedding?" She asked.

I looked at the clock and was surprised to see that it was already past 4:00. We were supposed to be at the wedding in just under an hour. Jenny grabbed her bag and headed to the bathroom, while I stayed in my room to get ready. 45 minutes later, Jenny finally emerged wearing the outfit she had chosen for the wedding. I found my eyes looking her up and down more than once. Damn, she looked good. Her hair was pulled back into a braid and she was wearing a yellow sundress with brown polka dots on it. The icing on top of the cake was the brown knee high cowboy boots she was wearing. This girl made country casual look absolutely incredible.

I found myself doubting the outfit I had picked out, which was a button up flannel top with a jean skirt and chucks. But the way Jenny's eyes lingered on me just a few seconds longer than usual as she told me that she liked my outfit choice made all of that doubt slip away. Before we could leave the house, my mom insisted on taking pictures of us together like we were two high schoolers going to prom. We posed for a few and then I ushered Jenny out of the house before my mom would embarrass me anymore.

When we arrived at the wedding, the ceremony had just ended and people were beginning to pour into the reception hall, which happened to be a barn in this case. We found the "DJ booth" set up and waiting for us. During the cocktail hour, we played some of the slower songs on the ipod's wedding playlist so we could save the exciting ones for when the reception actually started. When it was time for the wedding party to be introduced, Jenny and I each grabbed a microphone. I agreed to let her do the bridesmaid and groomsmen announcements so I could introduce the bride and groom. Jenny was a natural and I wondered if there was anything she couldn't do.

Toasts and dinner started right after the introductions. As soon as the guests had been served, Jeremiah's mom brought us each a plate filled with barbeque chicken, mashed potatoes, and green beans. I watched as Jenny brought the barbeque chicken to her mouth and then closed her eyes as she slowly ran her tongue along her bottom lip. I found my mind wandering to all of the other things she could do with that tongue… things such as licking ice cream or catching snowflakes of course.

Jenny must have caught me staring because she raised an eyebrow at me. "What? Do I have something on my face?"

I smiled and shook my head at her. "Nope. You're just the only girl I know who can somehow make barbeque chicken seductive."

She flashed me a cocky grin. "Maybe I just like driving you a little bit crazy." Before I could respond she reached out and touched one finger to my chin dimple. "But don't go getting all hot and bothered. I'm still not going home with you tonight."

I placed my hand on my chest in mock offense. "Of course not. What kind of girl do you think I am?"

"The kind that owns a High School Musical box set but somehow still convinces girls to go to bed with her?"

I crossed my arms in protest. "Hey now. You love my High School Musical box set. You were all over me and that box set."

Jenny shook her head at me and went back to teasing me with the barbeque chicken. We both finished our food quickly so we could focus on our plan for the night. As the servers were clearing the tables, we announced the father/daughter and mother/son dances.

As Jeremiah and his mom were dancing, Jenny turned to me with a serious look on her face. "Ok boss. What's the plan?"

I stroked my chin and looked up toward the ceiling. "We need to get as many people onto the dance floor as possible once this dance is over and then keep them out there. So we need to get the alcohol flowing and the feet moving."

"You are so corny. But I got your back. You pick out the song. I'm going start grabbing bottles of beer to hand to people as they come onto the dance floor." With that, Jenny was moving across the room and grabbing as many beers as she could.

I scrolled through the music on the ipod and stopped at "Chicken Fried" by Zac Brown Band. I mentally patted myself on the back for making such a good selection, then started the song right as the clapping from the mother/son dance was dying down.

I grabbed the microphone. "Alright everyone. It's

time to get up on the dance floor. I don't care if you grab your brother, mother, or significant other, just make sure you also grab a beer."

I watched Jenny roll her eyes at me while she handed out beers then went to grab more. Once she handed them out to all the guests who would accept, she brought one over to me and we clinked our bottles together. Jenny smiled and winked as her bottle tapped mine and I felt my stomach go into knots again. I grabbed the microphone and took it around the dance floor so everyone could take turns singing the chorus. Of course everyone knew the song because, well, small town Pennsylvania.

After the song ended, I switched to "Cotton Eye Joe."

"Alright," I announced, "Now that the liquid courage is flowing, it's time to really get those feet moving."

I grabbed Jenny's hand and dragged her out onto the dance floor. I started going through the moves and realized Jenny wasn't dancing with me.

I leaned close so she could hear me. "Not a fan?"

"I actually don't know this dance," Jenny admitted.

"What?!" I practically shouted. "This is my favorite line dance."

"You're a secret redneck, aren't you?" Jenny joked.

I took Jenny's hand in mine. "Oh honey. It's no

secret. You don't grow up in these here parts of Pennsylvania and walk away without a little redneck in you. Now let me put a little bit of this redneck inside of you."

Jenny's mouth quirked into a half smile due to my accidental sexual innuendo, but she quickly started mimicking my dance moves. As we danced together and stumbled over our feet, she threw her head back in laughter and I thought about how that might be my favorite sight in the whole world.

As the night dragged on, I continued shuffling through the songs that worked for each particular moment in the evening. About two hours into dancing, Jeremiah walked up to me and threw his arm around me like we were old friends.

"Rory my girl," he shouted much louder than was needed for how close we were standing to each other. "I can't thank you enough for doing this for me. You and your girl are awesome. I love you guys."

I decided not to correct him about the fact that Jenny wasn't my girl and just nodded my head.

Jeremiah pointed to Samantha and leaned closer to me like he was going to whisper, only his words came out at his normal speaking volume.

"You see that beautiful girl over there? Guess what?

She's pregnant with my child."

I tried my best to act surprised. I slapped Jeremiah on the back as I spoke. "That's awesome man!! Congrats!"

Jeremiah looked surprised at my response. "Thanks. Do you really think it's awesome?"

"Of course I do. You're going to be a dad. Aren't you excited?"

Jeremiah thought about it for a second. "Of course I am. I've always wanted to be a dad. But you're actually the only person who knows who has said it was awesome. Everyone else immediately pressured me to marry her and started asking us about money."

He paused and his face turned white. "Wait a second. You don't think I made a mistake marrying her, do you? Did I marry her just because people told me to?"

Just then, Samantha looked over at both of us from the dance floor. She did some move that looked like a crazy combination of the shopping cart and the sprinkler, only it didn't really resemble either of them too closely. When I looked at Jeremiah, he was staring at her like she was the greatest thing he had ever seen.

I put my hand on his shoulder. "Trust me. You didn't marry her just because people told you to. Sure, maybe you married her earlier than you originally planned, but you were always going to marry her. I mean look at you. Your wife is over there butchering the two oldest dance moves in the book and you are staring at her like she is a dancer on broadway. If that's not love, I don't know what is."

A huge smile spread across Jeremiah's face. "You're right. I love her more than anything else in this world and I already adore that baby too." He paused and then added, "She looks at you the same way, you know."

I gave Jeremiah a questioning look. "Who looks at me what way?"

"John's cousin over there." Just as he said it, Jenny turned and smiled at us. "You should see the way she stares at you when she doesn't think you're looking. She loves you."

Jeremiah was clearly drunk. He was talking nonsense now.

"Sorry to disappoint you buddy, but that's not love. We're not even together."

A shocked look came onto Jeremiah's face. "What?! No. You have to be together. You guys are in love and someday you will get married just like Samantha and I. And OH MY. You guys will make the most beautiful babies."

I reached across Jeremiah and grabbed the beer out of his hand. "Alright man. I think you've had enough. You can thank me tomorrow."

Jeremiah walked away and I looked over at Jenny who was already staring back at me. Jeremiah's words rang inside my head. Was there any chance he was right? No. Of course not. He was drunk. But why did that fact cause disappointment to course through me?

Chapter 5

I looked across the dinner table and noticed very loving eyes looking back at me. Those eyes said it all. She had fallen for me. How had I let this happen?

Actually, I knew exactly how it had happened. After Jeremiah and Samantha's wedding weekend, I immediately immersed myself back into the online dating scene. Something about that weekend had rocked me and I wanted to prove to myself that I was still the same old female slaying Rory. Within a week, I was messaging back and forth with Cara Seavers. In my hurry to date again, I didn't put my expectations out there from the beginning. After I realized that Cara was ending every text to me with heart emojis just two weeks after we started dating, I knew I had to be honest with her. I tried to tell her that this was just a fling and nothing serious, but I had trouble getting it through to her.

I should have cut it off there, but for some reason I felt the need to let it go on like this for another month and a half. Which brought me to the point I was at now where I had a lump the size of Texas in my throat while I stared across a table at a girl who was making love eyes at me. Cara wasn't even my usual type. She was barely 5'2" and had a short blonde bob with bangs that hung in front of her eyes. Don't get me wrong. She was a very pretty girl. Just not the kind of pretty girl that I happen to be attracted to.

I put my hand on top of hers and took a deep breath. "Listen Cara. You're an amazing girl and you're going to make someone really happy someday. I just have to be honest with you. You and I aren't looking for the same thing. I might not have articulated this well enough from the beginning, and I'm really sorry if that's the case, but I'm just not built for long term relationships. It's seriously not anything about you. It's all me."

I cringed as the words left my mouth. I had always vowed that I would never give the "it's not you, it's me" speech. Everyone knows that whenever someone says that, it totally has everything to do with the "You" they are talking to. Except in my case. I meant it.

I watched as Cara stared down at the table and prayed that those weren't tears that were forming at the corners of her eyes. As soon as my silent prayer was over, I saw one of those probable tears land on the counter. Shit. I had really done it this time.

"Please don't cry Cara," I begged. "I'm seriously not worth it. I spend way too much time working and most of my other time just doing nerdy things on my computer or watching some movie that was made for kids half my age."

Cara looked up at me and tried her best to put on a happy face, but the red rims around her eyes told another story.

She wiped her eyes on her shirt sleeve before starting to talk. "You don't have to apologize Rory. It's not your fault that you don't feel the same way. We can't control our feelings. Just like I couldn't control the fact that I was falling in love with you."

Falling in love? The words hit me like a ton of bricks and I sat there, unmoving, having no idea what to say.

Luckily, Cara found the words for me. "I'm going to go now. I'll just walk home. It's not far from here."

I still just sat there as Cara stood up and began walking toward the door. As she walked, her head slumped down and her shoulders rocked up and down. Great. She was crying again and it was all my fault.

I finally stood up and ran toward her, catching up right before she reached the door.

"Cara. Wait," I yelled as I grabbed ahold of her arm, not caring about the scene I was currently making in the restaurant. When she turned around, the tears were falling freely from her eyes and it took everything in me not to start crying myself. "Please take care of yourself, ok? And be safe on your walk home. And please be happy. Seriously Cara.

Please do everything you can to be happy. You deserve it."

Cara nodded slightly, then headed out the door. I did the walk of shame back to our table and quickly paid the bill.

Once I was in my car, my own tears started to fall. I hated hurting people. I don't think I had ever made someone else cry in my entire life and it was a terrible feeling. I could barely catch my breath and honestly thought I might hyperventilate. It's not like I didn't deserve it.

Before I could think it through, I was dialing Jenny's number. She picked up after just a few rings.

"Hey there pretty girl," she said cheerfully. "How is your Friday night going? Ryan and I decided to stay in and have a game night. We're both beat from work this week."

When I didn't say anything, Jenny spoke again. "Rory are you there? If you are, I can't hear anything that you're saying."

"Yeah. Sorry. I'm here," I just barely squeaked out.

A panic came over Jenny's voice. "Rory. What happened? Are you ok? Are you hurt? Did you have an accident?"

The worry in her voice strangely cheered me up a little and I was finally able to get a few more words out. "No. I'm fine Jenny. Sorry to worry you. I just had a really bad night."

"What's up girly? Talk to me."

I shook my head, even though I knew she couldn't actually see me. "That's the thing - I can't. This falls under the category of things we shouldn't talk about."

Jenny sighed into the phone. "I don't care about the stupid rule. You need me right now so I'm going to be here for you. Tell me what happened."

I let the whole story spill out from our chats online to the awful dinner I had just endured, ending with her admitting that she was falling in love with me. I started to cry again as I told the story.

"I broke her heart Jenny. I've never done that to a girl before. I said I never would. I'm a terrible person. God, I'm so awful."

"You don't really believe this is the first time you broke a girl's heart, do you?" Jenny asked.

"Well, yeah. All of my flings end really cordially. Heck, I'm even friends with some of those girls still."

Jenny let out a sympathetic laugh. "Rory, you're a certified ten with loads of money who treats girls like royalty. You can't honestly believe it's not heartbreaking when you end things."

I glared into the phone. "Is this supposed to be helpful? Because right now you're just making me feel worse."

"That's not what I'm trying to do," Jenny explained. "I'm just saying, you're an amazing person Rory. You're caring, funny, and insanely generous. Not to mention, you are pretty much the most beautiful human being on this planet both inside and out. You're going to break some hearts whether you mean to or not. That doesn't mean you're a bad person. It just means that people realize how great you are and how lucky they would be to have you in their lives."

Jenny's words started to make me feel a little better. I couldn't say that I believed them at that moment, but it still felt good to hear her say it.

"Thanks Jenny," I said sincerely. "I just don't know how I'm supposed to go back to my apartment and sit there over the next few weeks being reminded of this girl who is now hurting really badly thanks to me."

"Ok. A few things," Jenny lectured. "First of all, you sound like you're the one who got dumped. Also, you are giving yourself way too much credit acting like this girl is going to sit around crying for weeks. I shouldn't have said all those nice things about you and let them go to your head. Let's be honest - you're not *that* great."

I rolled my eyes and tried to think of a good comeback, but Jenny wasn't done. "I also have an idea. You sound like you need to get away. You've been telling me lately that you really need to plan the trip to see your dad. Just do it. Cancel meetings and come sometime this week. The bonus is that your favorite person in the world lives in LA and if you come now, we can do some early birthday celebrations."

I heard a muffled voice in the background, then Jenny added, "You should ask Todd if he wants to come with you. I feel like the four of us could get into some trouble together."

I considered everything she was saying. My dad was agreeable to seeing me anytime when I was the one traveling to him and Todd was a high school math teacher so he wouldn't be starting work again for a few weeks. Plus, it would be awesome if Jenny and I could celebrate our 25th birthdays together. My birthday was August 27 and hers was just a few days later on September 3rd.

"I'm in as long as I'm home by the 27th. I always spend my birthday with my mom. Let me just talk to my dad and Todd and I'll get back to you."

I quickly called my dad and Todd and before I knew it all of the plans were made and the plane tickets had been bought.

Just three days after my mental breakdown, Todd and I were boarding a plane. The plan was to stay at my dad's house for the next week but to spend as much time as possible with Jenny as well. Yes, I was flying to Los Angeles to spend time with the girl who had inadvertently started this whole chain of events, but whatever.

As we waited for the plane to take off, Todd turned to me. "Ok, let's make a little deal. I won't embarrass you in front of Jenny if you don't embarrass me in front of Ryan."

I threw my head back in laughter, then stuck out my hand. "Deal. I won't tell your wannabe lover boy that you have been stalking him on social media ever since I told you Jenny was moving in with him."

Todd stuck his tongue out at me. "And I won't tell Jenny that you are secretly in love with her."

I gave him a playful punch in the arm. "Even though that's not true anyway, I still appreciate it."

After picking up our baggage and the keys to our rental car, I stepped outside and took a deep breath. "This weather is fantastic. I love California. Seriously, have I mentioned just how much I love LA?"

Todd smiled over at me. "Just about every single time you come to visit. But I must say, I'm very happy that my first trip here is with a California groupie."

We pulled up to my dad's house about an hour later and I smiled at the sight. "Is it weird that this feels like home? I could probably count on one hand the number of times I've stayed in this house and with the amount my dad and I talk, we're practically strangers. But something about being here just always feels right."

Todd shrugged his shoulders. "You love California and things you love always feel like home."

I put my arm around Todd and pulled him close. "Having you here with me makes it feel even more like home."

Before I had the chance to knock, my dad opened the door. He put his arms out and pulled me in close.

"My baby girl," he shouted into my ear. "How long has it been? Almost a year? You look so much older and more mature than the last time I saw you."

He pulled away and looked into my eyes, with tears forming in his own. "I've missed you so much honey. I'm sorry I didn't get back to Pennsylvania for any holidays. I promise I'll do better."

I almost spoke up and told him that he shouldn't make promises he can't keep, but I just leaned in and gave him a kiss on the cheek instead. I hated to see a grown man cry and I worried that if I called him out on being an absentee father, he might have a full on meltdown.

My dad's house was a modest size three bedroom

with two bathrooms. One of the extra rooms was designated as my room and the few times I visited, he encouraged me to decorate it however I wanted. The other room was a guest room. My dad's house was a lot like my mom's in that he had framed pictures of us all over the place. I was always surprised to see how many he had. He honestly must have hung up every picture we've ever taken together. His refrigerator was covered with every article ever written about my social media platform.

"So, what's the plan?" My dad asked. "I am off the rest of the night and don't go back in until tomorrow at 4:00pm."

If I was honest, I had absolutely no idea what my dad's job was. All I knew was that he worked strange hours and used to travel all of the time when I was growing up.

I looked at the clock and saw that it was 6:00. No wonder I felt so hungry. It was already 9:00 on the east coast.

"I'm in desperate need of some food, but let me call Jenny quick to see what her plans are."

As I was walking away with my phone in hand, I heard Todd whisper something to my dad about my "girlfriend."

"Hey California girl," Jenny answered on the other end of the phone. "Finally landed on the best coast?"

"I have," I said as a goofy grin spread across my face. "And I'm not going to disagree with you on that one you know. Perfect weather, beautiful scenery, pretty girls - it doesn't get much better than that."

"Pretty girls, huh? See anything you like so far?" The flirtation in Jenny's voice wasn't lost on me and as usual it set my body on fire.

"If you're asking if I've found any girls that are prettier than you, the answer is obviously no." And I wasn't kidding. I was truly convinced that there weren't any girls in this world prettier than Jenny.

"My oh my Miss Montgomery. I would say that flattery won't get you anywhere, but that's a lie. It will get you everywhere."

"Everywhere, huh?" I could think of quite a few places I would like flattery to get me if I was channeling my inner 18 year old boy.

"You're bad," Jenny joked. "But I think I'll still keep you around. Speaking of, when do I get to see you?"

"I'd love to say tonight, but I know you have to get up early for work tomorrow and I should spend time around here with my dad anyway. So how about tomorrow when you get off work?"

"Sounds wonderful. How do you feel about dinner

and clubbing in West Hollywood?"

Just thinking about clubbing with Jenny was enough to get my heart racing. "I feel great about that. I should go for now, but text me with more details."

"I will," Jenny promised. "And Rory?"

"Yeah?"

"I'm really excited to see you."

I felt like I could burst from happiness just from those simple words. "I'm really excited to see you too Wedding Jenny," I tried to say as nonchalantly as possible.

When I walked back to the kitchen where my dad and Todd were, they were both laughing and staring at me.

"So," my dad said while lifting an eyebrow. "Tell me about this Jenny girl."

I rolled my eyes. "Well, no matter what Todd tries to tell you, she's not my girlfriend. We're just friends."

My dad's grin widened. "He told me you'd say that."

I shook my head at both of them. "That's because it's true."

"If you say so, then I believe you," my dad conceded, but him and Todd continued to elbow each other like they were two teenage boys sharing an inside joke.

I changed the subject by asking what we were having for dinner and my dad offered to make steak and potatoes on the grill. We spent the rest of the night laughing and catching up and luckily, avoiding the topic of Jenny.

The next day, my dad took us to a local flea market where we shopped and ate just about everything. Around 3:00, we headed home so my dad could get ready and go to work.

"I'm working until midnight and then have to be back in at 8 tomorrow morning, so I probably won't see you until tomorrow night," my dad informed me as he was leaving the house. Before the door completely shut, he leaned his head back in and added, "How about I make reservations for us and your friends to go to dinner? There's also someone that I'd like you to meet."

I nodded my head, taken back by my dad's question. He slipped out the door and I stood there running his words back through my mind. Someone he wants me to meet? He had to be talking about a girlfriend because who else would he want me to meet? I wasn't sure how to feel about this realization. Unlike my mom, who hadn't dated at all since the divorce, I always figured my dad was dating people. Who else would he be spending all of his free time with when it clearly wasn't his own daughter? Still, he had never dated anyone seriously enough to feel the need introduce them to me and I didn't know how to feel about this being the case now. I guess I shouldn't care. It's not like I had some irrational dream of my parents getting back together. It also wouldn't be weird seeing my dad happy with someone other than my mom because, honestly, I had never really seen my parents happy around each other. Sure there were a few vacations or holidays where they actually acted friendly towards each other, but even then I had never even seen them kiss or hold hands. Still, it felt strange to think about. Did she have kids? Had he met her kids? A lump formed in my stomach as I thought about him actually spending time with these kids. That's when it hit me that this was what bothered me. I wanted my dad to be happy, but I didn't want someone else's kids to get the time and attention that I should have gotten from him. That might be selfish but I didn't care.

I tried to shake all of these thoughts from my head so I could get ready for my night out, but still texted Jenny to tell her that there was something I wanted to talk to her about. Immediately after, my phone started to ring and I saw it was her.

"Is everything ok?" She asked before I even had the chance to say hello.

"Yeah, it was just something that my dad said that I wanted to run past you. But I'd rather talk about it in person if that's ok," I admitted.

"Of course," Jenny agreed. "I hope it's ok, but my best friend and her fiancé are actually going to go to dinner with us. They live in Santa Monica so it's not a long trip and I've told her about you so she's been begging to meet you."

"You've told her about me, huh?" I asked with a hint of flirtation in my voice, but I could feel my face turning red at the thought of Jenny telling her friend about me.

"Of course. She knows all about the pretty girl from Pennsylvania with the cute little chin dimple," Jenny admitted nonchalantly.

I laughed and told her that I was excited to meet her friend, but had to get ready. The truth was that sometimes Jenny's flirtation was too much for me and I had to take a step back and remind myself that it didn't mean anything to either of us. Because it didn't. It was just some simple flirting. Nothing more.

Two hours later, we were standing in front of a cute little Italian restaurant, being introduced to all of Jenny's friends. Ryan was even better looking in person. He had shaggy blonde hair and tanned skin that screamed California boy. He was wearing khaki shorts with a red polo shirt and boat shoes. Jenny's best friend, Allison, was tall with the build of a basketball player and her fiancé, Bret, was even taller. They both had blonde hair and firm bodies. They looked like the type of couple that went to the gym together everyday and whose dates revolve around physical activity such as rock climbing or hiking. Or maybe in California surfing was more likely.

Jenny was wearing a pair of short jean shorts that hugged her curves perfectly and a low cut t-shirt. She had on big sunglasses and when she took them off the setting California sun made her eyes shimmer even more than usual. I stepped closer and gave her a big hug, holding on a little longer than usual. I couldn't help but notice that Jenny wasn't in any hurry to pull away either. When we finally backed up from each other, every other member of our group was staring at us and Todd had that look on his face that said "I know you're totally in love with her." I gave him a warning glance and his face went straight.

"So, shall we head in?" Jenny asked, hip checking me as we walked in next to each other.

Not long into dinner, I felt like we were surrounded by old friends. I learned that Allison and Jenny had been friends since high school and had also attended the same college, which is where Allison met Bret their freshman year. He had proposed about a year ago and they were doing a small wedding with close friends and family in Miami on new year's eve.

I told Allison how much I enjoyed Miami and a smile spread across her face as she looked between Jenny and I. "Jenny you should totally bring Rory as your plus one." She looked over at me and added with a wink, "I can't call it a date because Jenny is afraid of that word."

Jenny gave her friend an annoyed look and I couldn't tell if she was mad about the date comment or the fact that she had suggested bringing me.

I squeezed her leg in reassurance. "Don't worry. You don't have to take me. I know it's not your thing."

Jenny's face relaxed as she smiled over at me. "I honestly didn't even know I was getting a plus one. I figured only people in serious relationships would."

Allison interrupted, "Of course you get a plus one. You're my best friend and pretty much vice maid of honor after my sister."

I elbowed Jenny in the side. "So, you pretty much take over if the maid of honor can't fulfill her duties?"

"No. She actually has all of the maid of honor duties without the actual title. My little sister is pretty much useless, but would also murder me in my sleep if I didn't make her my maid of honor," Allison admitted.

Jenny looked at me and lifted an eyebrow. "So, what do you say? Any interest in coming with me? It could be fun.

Although, I feel like I should warn you that I will be busy fulfilling my vice MOH duties, so you might be spending a decent chunk of time alone."

I acted like I was considering the offer even though I knew there was nothing to think about. It was a weekend in Miami and a chance to spend more time with Jenny. Of course I was going to accept.

"I'm not the type of girl to turn down a weekend in Miami. I'm in. And don't worry about me. I'll make friends. Incase you didn't notice, I'm pretty charming."

"Oh I noticed," Jenny said giving me a half smile.

The rest of the dinner was spent talking about Ryan's nonprofit and what plans he had for the kids. I noticed Todd was hanging on every word he was saying and thought I was going to have to remind him not to drool.

After dinner, we said goodbye to Allison and Bret and headed to one of the bigger clubs in West Hollywood. That's when the alcohol started flowing. As soon as we got in, Ryan bought shots for all of us. After that, I chugged down a very strong mixed drink, before ordering another round of shots. Normally I didn't drink so much so quickly. I was the type of person who liked to have the "constant buzz." The type that was just enough to let loose, but not enough to do anything stupid and I had a feeling that tonight was quickly headed toward stupid.

After exploring the bar and having a few more drinks, we made our way onto the dance floor. With liquid courage pouring through me, I pulled Jenny close to me.

I stood behind her with my hands on her hips, while she danced up against me. If I hadn't been drunk to start, her dancing would have pushed me over the edge. She was intoxicating. Between the smell that graced my nose as her hair wisped in front of my face and the feel of her curves tight against my body, I felt like I had entered a whole other world; a world where it was only me and Jenny; a world where we could do and feel anything; a world where I wasn't afraid to follow my heart.

Before I could even begin to consider where these thoughts were coming from, I took Jenny's arm and twisted her around so she was facing me. I continued to dance up close to her, resting my head on her forehead while our bodies moved together in perfect synchronization. I found myself staring down at her lips and wondering what would happen if I closed the distance between us.

Jenny's eyes fluttered from my eyes down to my own lips and I wondered if she was having the same thoughts. If she was, she probably wouldn't mind if I moved in close and… suddenly I felt a finger on my lips. I looked up to see

Jenny smiling at me and shaking her head playfully. I kissed the finger she had placed on my lips then used my hand to guide it back to her lips. I couldn't tell whether the look on her face was due to lust or surprise, but I took her hand and intertwined her fingers with mine anyway. When she didn't try to stop me, I decided to move in for the kiss again. As I moved in close, she closed her eyes and I noticed a lustful sigh leaving her lips. When my lips were just about an inch from hers, Jenny unwound her fingers from mine and gently pushed away from me.

She leaned in close so I could hear her words. "Could we talk *please*?" The way she emphasized the word please made me feel like she was either upset or angry and I started cursing myself out as I followed her out of the bar.

Once we were out on the sidewalk and away from the noise, Jenny stopped to look at me, crossing her arms. "What is going on with you Rory? I realize you're drunk right now, but this isn't like you. Does this have anything to do with what you said you wanted to talk to me about?"

I tried to think of the right words to say, but before I could string a sentence together, I broke down into tears. Jenny immediately pulled me into a tight hug and rubbed my back.

She whispered into my ear. "Hey, it's ok. What's

going on? Tell me what's wrong."

I wasn't even sure what I was crying about until the words subconsciously spilled out of my mouth. "Today... When my dad was leaving for work..." I took a deep breath trying to will myself to stop crying so the words could come out. "He told me that there is someone he wants me to meet. He wants to bring this person to dinner with all of us tomorrow. It has to be a woman right? Like, he must be dating someone and it must be serious if he wants me to meet her. And the thing is, I don't really care about that. My dad is a grown man with his own life. He can do what he wants. But then I started thinking. What if she has kids? What if he treats those kids like they're his own? But like his own kids that he actually spends time with? Kids that he takes to the movies or to a football game. Kids that he calls up just to ask how their day is going. What if he actually spends holidays with these kids? What if he wakes them up Christmas morning and they make Christmas cookies and watch Christmas movies?"

With that last sentence, the tears started streaming down my face again. Jenny rested her forehead against mine and gently ran her hand through my hair.

"Hey, hey," Jenny whispered soothingly. "Just try to breathe, ok? Everything is going to be ok."

Once I had calmed down, Jenny backed up and looked into my eyes while wiping away the stray tears that were still running down my cheeks.

"Ok. Let me make sure I have this straight," she said calmly. "Your dad told you that there is someone he wants you to meet and he is bringing this person to dinner tomorrow?"

I nodded slowly and wiped my face with the back of my arm, finally willing the tears to stop.

"Ok. Did he say anything else?"

I shook my head no, still unable to form words at the moment.

"Alright…" Jenny spoke slowly as though she was trying not to upset me anymore. "I agree. It does sound like he is dating someone. Now, I'm not trying to push aside your feelings, but I think you should wait to hear all of the details before jumping to conclusions. She might not have any kids. Heck, this 'she' we're talking about, might not actually exist. It's not worth getting yourself upset about now though because you might be getting upset about nothing. But, you know, if you find out there is an actual reason to be upset then I'll be here for you. I mean it Ror. Now what do you say we get some food and water in your stomach?"

I followed her down the street until we came to a

small pizza shop where she ordered us each a slice of cheese pizza and a bottle of water. After I chugged my whole bottle, she tossed me hers.

"Take it," she said with a wink. "You need it more than me."

By the time we were done eating, I had sobered up a decent amount. I looked up at the clock and realized it was already 1:30am.

"Shit," I said while looking around and taking in my surroundings. "We left Todd and Ryan awhile ago. We need to get back to the bar before they start to get worried."

To be honest, I had completely forgotten about Todd and Ryan. Once I started dancing with Jenny, I forgot anyone else in the world existed. As we walked back to the bar, I silently scolded myself for being such a terrible best friend.

I looked around for Todd once we were back inside the bar, but Jenny spotted them first.

She nudged me in the side and pointed across the bar. "Yeah, I don't think they were too worried about us."

I followed the direction of her finger with my eyes and found Ryan and Todd across the bar having a full on sloppy make out session. Jenny and I laughed as we made our way over to them.

Once we got to them, the make out was still going

strong so I leaned close to Todd's ear.

"Having fun?" I asked.

Todd jumped in the air to the sound of my voice, tearing his lips away from Ryan. Jenny and I laughed and she threw her hand up for a high five.

Ryan shook his head, but I could tell he was laughing. "You guys are jerks."

"Yeah. You scared me to death," Todd added.

"It's not my fault you were too busy to be paying attention to your best friend," I said with a laugh.

Todd looked over at me to say something else and I noticed he couldn't keep eye contact and was swaying back and forth.

I put my hand on his shoulder. "Ok buddy. I think it's time we get you home."

He pushed his lip out and gave me his best pouty face. "Oh calm down," I scolded. "The bar is about to close anyway."

As we made our way outside to our rideshare, I noticed that Ryan had taken Todd's hand. I looked over at Jenny and raised an eyebrow and she just shrugged her shoulders and smiled.

When our ride arrived, Todd pulled Ryan close and they shared another kiss before Todd flung himself into the car. Before I got in I turned back to Jenny and squeezed her hand.

"I'm really sorry about what happened earlier. I never should have…"

Before I could finish, Jenny interrupted me. "Hey. We'll talk about it tomorrow, ok? Just go home and get some sleep."

Sleep was unlikely. A night full of worry was more like it. I hoped and prayed that Jenny could forgive me for what I had done or at least what I had wanted to do. I also wished I could forget about how it felt to have my lips so close to hers.

Chapter 6

The next day I was awoken to the sound of my phone ringing. I blinked my eyes at the screen a few times and noticed it was Jenny calling.

"He-hello?" I said, just barely able to get the words out.

"Hey sleepy head," Jenny said cheerfully. "Am I seriously waking you up? Do you know what time it is?"

I pulled the phone away from my ear and blinked at it again, until I could read the time on the clock - 12:00 pm. I jumped out of bed. How had I slept so late? I guess it could have something to do with all of the tossing and turning I did last night. The tossing and turning I had done because… oh no. The memories flooded back to me. Shots, lots of shots, followed by some sexy grinding and then the worst part. I tried to kiss Jenny, not just once, but twice. As if that wasn't bad enough, I had followed it up by bawling onto her shoulder.

"Hey, are you still there?" Jenny asked from the other end of the phone.

"Yeah. Sorry. I was just thinking about last night," I admitted. "I really am sorry Jenny."

"Hey, let's talk about it in a few minutes, ok? Ryan

and I are on our way over to your dad's house with some hangover food for you guys."

"On your way over?" I tried to ask nonchalantly while I desperately rustled through my closet. "How do you know the address?"

"Todd gave it to Ryan last night," Jenny said with a laugh.

I rolled my eyes. "Of course he did. Speak of the devil, I better go make sure that fool is alive."

"Ok. We'll see you guys in about 20 minutes."

I threw on clothes and rushed out of my room to find Todd sitting at the kitchen bar, still looking half asleep. I hit him in the back of the head.

"Wake up," I shouted. "Your boyfriend is on his way over here."

Todd almost fell to the ground as he jumped out of his chair. "What?! Why wouldn't you tell me sooner?"

"Because I just found out. *Someone* gave Ryan our address last night so they were already on their way over here when they called about 5 minutes ago." I took a moment to take in Todd's disheveled appearance and added, "Do you even remember what happened last night?"

"Of course I do," Todd said smugly. "It was one of the best nights of my life."

"Wow. You're super gay," I joked while sticking my tongue out at him. "Now, go get ready."

When Todd was almost out of the room, he turned around and gave me a goofy smile. "By the way, I saw you getting up close and personal with your girl. Did you guys…?"

"Nothing happened and I don't want to talk about it," I interrupted sternly.

Todd took the hint and left the room without saying another word. About 15 minutes later, I heard a knock on the door. I took a deep breath before answering, nervous about seeing Jenny. If Jenny felt any awkwardness over the previous night's events, she didn't show it as she pulled me into a tight hug as soon as they were through the door. She gave me an extra squeeze before letting go to say hi to Todd who had now made his way over to us.

I directed everyone toward the kitchen, where Jenny presented the buffalo wings and French fries they had brought for lunch.

"Perfect hangover cure for those East Coasters who can't handle a little West Hollywood partying," Jenny announced with a cocky grin.

"Hey! Don't lump me in with my friend. I'm not actually hungover," I pointed out.

"And that couldn't have anything to do with the pretty girl who made sure you had water and pizza last night now could it?" Jenny raised a seductive eyebrow as she asked the question.

I smiled back at her. "I have absolutely no idea what you're talking about."

After we were done eating, the boys suggested watching a movie and took a seat next to each other on the couch. They scrolled through Netflix and chose a documentary about some gay athlete they both liked. Before I could sit down, I felt a hand on my shoulder. I turned around to find Jenny standing close to me.

"Since this movie wasn't made for girls in middle school, I'm sure you're not super into it. So do you think you would go for a walk with me?" She asked.

I agreed and told Todd he better behave while I was gone.

"You too," he said with a smirk.

Once we were a few steps away from the house, Jenny turned to look at me. "Are you ok?" She asked. "I've been worried about you."

"Worried about me? Why?" I asked dumbly. Clearly she was referring to my breakdown in the middle of the street.

"You were really upset last night. I've never seen you like that." The sincerity behind her voice was so sweet that it made my heart race.

I sighed. "I'm ok. I think my emotions were on overdrive because of the alcohol." I hesitated, then added, "Listen Jenny. I really am sorry about how I acted in the bar. I know it's no excuse, but I drank way too much way too quickly. Then we got to dancing and I guess that's just what I'm used to doing when I dance with a pretty girl in a bar."

"So, is that all it was?" Jenny asked. "You got carried away and forgot who you were dancing with?"

I couldn't tell by Jenny's voice if she would be relieved or upset if that were the case, but I knew I couldn't lie to her.

I looked down at the ground and kicked around a rock. "No. I knew exactly who I was dancing with. I was very aware of who I was trying to kiss. That moment wasn't about just wanting to kiss someone. In that moment, all I wanted was to kiss you."

I held my breath, worried about what Jenny might say to that. I knew this kind of honesty could get me in trouble and hoped it wouldn't ruin our friendship.

Jenny nudged me in the side. "Hey pretty girl, look at me. You don't have to be embarrassed. I wanted to kiss you too. Heck, I almost did. But one of us had to stop it before we did something we would regret."

I wanted to tell her that I didn't honestly think I could ever regret kissing her, but decided it was for the best if I didn't.

"Maybe we should just do it once. You know, get it out of our systems," I said only half joking.

Jenny laughed. "That does seem like the easier and more fun solution, doesn't it? I like what you and I have though. I don't want us to become friends with benefits who eventually have a falling out."

I nodded my head. I knew she was right. I mean what did I really expect to happen if we kissed? That we would ride into the sunset and live happily ever after? Of course not. That's not what either of us wanted. The best case scenario would be that we did become some sort of friends with benefits and I finally got to fulfill my fantasies about Jenny, but I felt like she deserved better than that. Plus, I feared the worst case scenario where a physical relationship complicated what we had and things fell apart. I didn't want that.

We walked in silence for a few minutes before Jenny spoke again. "You don't talk about your dad much," she pointed out.

I sighed and looked up at the blue California sky. "There's not much to say. My dad. He's a good person. He means well and I adore him. But he's a terrible father."

"I'm sorry," Jenny said sincerely, a hint of pain behind her voice.

"It's ok. It was honestly never that hard for me because it's always been the norm. Even before my parents' divorce, my dad traveled all the time for work and missed a lot of my big events. I'm used to him not being around. I guess I just always told myself that it's just how he is and that was enough. But the thought of him being with someone who could possibly have kids was too much for me. Like I said, I can deal with him not winning any dad of the year awards. I wouldn't be able to deal with it if I knew he was a better dad to someone else. Then it would no longer be about him and his own parenting problems. It would be about me and why I wasn't good enough."

"Hey," Jenny said taking my hands in hers. "No matter what happens, it doesn't mean that you're not good enough. You are more than good enough Rory. You're spectacular. And judging by the decor in your dad's house, I'd say that he most certainly realizes that, but if he doesn't, it's his loss. Honestly, I feel bad for *him* for the little time he's spent with you. He sure is missing out."

"Do you really mean that?" I asked, while trying to stop the tears from returning.

"Of course I do," Jenny answered sincerely. "Rory you light up every room you walk into. There's something truly special about you. Whenever I talk to you, my day gets a thousand times better. You have a way of making people feel invincible. That's how you make me feel at least."

With those words, the desire to kiss Jenny came back just as strongly as last night. Only this time there was no alcohol involved. I also knew that I had to clear those thoughts from my head.

"So, your parents…" Jenny started, bringing my thoughts back to the present. "Are they the reason you hate love?"

"Just for the record, I don't hate love. I actually love love and I love loving people. I love seeing other people in love too actually. Give me a romantic comedy any day. Make my life a romantic comedy? No thanks. But to answer your question, yes, my parents are the reason I don't do long term relationships. They were miserable with each other. I know that's not always the case, but I don't want to risk it. I don't want to spend my whole life just tolerating someone. Life is such an adventure and I feel like my parents missed out on truly living because they were so focused on hating each other."

Jenny nodded in understanding. "That makes sense. What about kids? Would you still consider having any on your own?"

"I've thought about it. I love kids and would love to raise my own. But I haven't decided if it's something I'd want to take on alone. My mom practically did it alone and she did a great job, but I know it took a ton out of her. What about you?" I asked.

Jenny lifted one shoulder and let it drop. "I love kids too and if I was going to go the marriage route, I would definitely want at least three. But I don't think I could do it on my own. I think I'll just be the cool aunt that spoils her nieces and nephews rotten."

"And why are *you* so against relationships?" I inquired. "It doesn't seem to have anything to do with your family, unless I'm missing something."

"No. My family is actually the epitome of what relationships should be. My parents have been disgustingly in love for 35 years. My 27 year old brother is already married with two kids and my sister is only 23 and has been with her boyfriend for almost ten years. I'm the black sheep of the family."

"So, what's the reason?" I tried asking again,

realizing that Jenny was avoiding the topic.

"I really don't want to talk about it," Jenny said sternly, before adding, "Ever."

"I get it," I conceded. "No worries. Shall we get back to the boys?"

Jenny agreed and although I had said I would drop it, the only thing I could think about our whole walk home was what could have possibly happened to turn Jenny away from relationships.

We spent the rest of the afternoon hanging out, playing board games until my dad got home. As soon as he entered the house, he introduced himself to Jenny and Ryan and made small talk for a few minutes before asking to speak with me privately. As I walked past Jenny to join him in the other room, she reached out and gave my hand a gentle squeeze. I gave her an appreciative smile, thinking that she couldn't possibly realize how much her small gestures meant to me.

Once we were in another room and out of ear shot my dad turned to me, with a nervous look on his face. Instead of talking, he began running his hand through his short brown hair, which was a nervous habit of his.

"So listen," he said, clearing his throat before continuing. "I'm sorry about running off to work right after I told you there was someone I wanted you to meet. I was worried about how you would react. It was selfish and cowardly of me."

I waited for him to say something else and when I realized he wasn't going to, I decided to speak up.

"So, who is it that you want to me to meet?" I tried to ask as nonchalantly as possible.

"Her name is Monica Pearl. She's my age and we've..ah..we've been seeing each other for about a year now."

"Oh," was all I was able to say. I knew this was coming, but I hadn't thought about a logical response.

"Yeah," my dad said tentatively. "She has become the most important person in my life, after you of course, so it was very important for you two to meet."

I wanted to question whether I really was more important than her. I'm sure he spent holidays with her. I'm sure he saw her more than once a year and that they actually spoke to each other on a regular basis. But I had decided a long time ago that this wasn't a battle I wanted to fight with my dad.

When I didn't say anything, my dad continued. "I hope you don't mind that I invited her to a dinner with your friends. I just thought it might be, you know, less awkward for you this way."

"No, you were right. I appreciate that," I said with a sincere smile because he was right. As awkward as this meeting was going to be, I figured it would be even worse if it were just the three of us sitting around a table trying to make small talk. My dad was practically a stranger to me so throwing another, actual stranger, into the mix would just be weird.

"Ok. Well good talk," my dad said while awkwardly patting me on the shoulder. "And Rory?"

"Yes Dad?"

"You do know that I love you, right?"

I squeezed his arm while giving him a genuine smile. "Yeah Dad. I know."

About a half hour later, we were all squeezing into my dad's SUV to head to the restaurant where Monica was going to meet us. When we arrived, she was waiting for us by the entrance. The first thing I noticed about her was that she was pretty much the opposite of my mom. She was short and on the curvy side without actually being fat and she had wavy blonde hair that fell down to about her shoulders. I then noticed that she had a genuine smile on her face and seemed sincerely happy to meet me as my dad introduced her to each of us.

Once we were seated at our table, the conversation flowed fairly easily with everyone contributing equally. Not long into dinner, Jenny spoke directly to Monica.

"So Monica," she questioned, "Do you have any kids?"

I passed her an appreciative smile and lightly squeezed her hand. She smiled back at me knowing she had asked the question that had been burning in my mind all night.

"No, I don't actually," Monica said. "I always just focused on my nieces and nephews rather than having any of my own."

I noticed that she chose her words carefully, not wanting to incriminate herself. She clearly realized that saying she didn't want kids would be like saying she didn't want the package that came along with my dad. Even though I already had a mother and wasn't looking for another one, it still meant something to me that she would be so careful about this. I also breathed a sigh of relief knowing that all my worries about my dad having this whole other family were unwarranted. Beside me, Jenny gave me a smile that said *see I told you there was nothing to worry about*. The rest of the dinner went smoothly and I was happy when my dad and Monica said goodbye rather than trying to prolong this meeting even longer.

We got back to the house a little after nine and my dad asked if Jenny and Ryan wanted to stick around for a little while longer.

"I'd really like the chance to get to know Rory's friends a little better," he confessed, but by the way he looked at Jenny when he said it, I had a feeling he really wanted to figure out what her deal was. I wasn't sure if he was playing the protective father role since Todd had convinced him we were together or if he was just curious to learn more about the girl I had grown so close to over the past year. Either way, I appreciated it.

Once they were able to talk more one on one, Jenny and my dad got along really well. They quickly got into a back and forth banter, which actually wasn't very surprising given how similar my personality was to my dad's. I could tell Jenny was hesitant to like him though, like it was against the friend code to like the man who had broken his own daughter's heart.

Around midnight, Jenny yawned and raised her hands over her head, announcing that they should go. Todd and Ryan had already fallen asleep snuggled up under a blanket on the couch, so Jenny gently woke them up. I just stood there rolling my eyes at Todd, shocked at how quickly my best friend had become a big pile of mush.

My dad said goodbye to everyone and Ryan walked out to the car in a tired stupor, while Todd made his way up to bed. Once we were on the front porch just the two of us, Jenny turned toward me.

"So your dad is...nice," she said hesitantly.

"You don't have to do that, you know," I corrected her. "You don't have to worry about saying nice things. Like I said, I know my dad is a good guy."

"You're a lot like him, you know," she said relaxing a bit. "You have his humor and his charm."

"I just hope I don't inherit his tendency to disappear from people's lives," I admitted, wondering if that's what I did with the girls I dated. I didn't think it was. Even though I was always the one to end things, I did try to keep in touch and I always meant it when I said I would be there if they ever needed me.

"You didn't," Jenny reassured me. "You're a lot like your mom too. Plus, the combination of genetics that they gave you in the looks department is on point."

As I laughed, we looked over toward Jenny's car where Ryan was passed out in the front seat.

"I guess I should probably get sleeping beauty home," she said reluctantly.

I pulled her in close before I could over think it and whispered in her ear. "Thanks for being such a good friend to me. You really do get me."

"Hey, what are.. friends for?" She whispered back. I couldn't help but notice that she had hesitated on the word friend, but decided not to think into it too much.

Chapter 7

The rest of my time in LA flew by, with me spending as much time as possible with my dad and Jenny when they weren't working. My dad had also brought Monica around two more times and I had to admit that I did like her. She was carefree and down to earth and honestly seemed like a much better fit for my dad than my mom ever was. I didn't mean that in a bad way towards my mom. She just had a much more serious approach to life and while her and I balanced each other out in that way, it just caused her and my dad to butt heads.

I couldn't believe how fast our last night in LA came around. It was a Friday night so we had planned to use this as the night to celebrate our birthdays. I had already said goodbye to my dad earlier in the day because his work schedule was going to keep me from seeing him before we left. Around 6:00, Todd and I called a rideshare to take us to a restaurant in West Hollywood. The plan was the same as the last weekend's - dinner and then out for drinks. I had vowed to myself that I wasn't going to drink as much this time, but apparently Jenny had not made the same vow. By the time we met them for dinner, she already had a buzz going. I nursed one glass of wine during dinner while she quickly chugged down three.

By the time we got to the club, she was definitely drunk and I decided that was even more of a reason for me to take it easy. I wanted to make sure I could take care of her if it became necessary. Soon we were out on the dance floor and Ryan and Todd quickly got into a pattern of switching between dancing and whispering to each other and sharing steamy make out sessions.

I tried to keep my dancing with Jenny a little more pg this time around to keep myself from feeling tempted to make any moves. At some point during the night, she had draped her arms over my shoulders and was now holding me tight. I wasn't sure if she was doing this to keep herself upright or if she just wanted feel close to me. I figured it was probably a combination of both, but either way, I wasn't complaining.

I felt my body heating up as Jenny leaned even closer to me to whisper in my ear. "You look really pretty tonight," she confessed. "Like ridiculously pretty. My God Rory, I think you might be the most beautiful person on this planet."

I wanted to tell her that she was wrong, because that person was actually her. But in that moment, I couldn't find the words. Luckily, I didn't have to. Jenny apparently wasn't done whispering her confessions to me.

"You don't understand how hard it is to keep myself from kissing you right now," she admitted.

This time I did respond. "Oh I think I understand completely."

Before this back and forth could go any further, I felt a tap on my shoulder. It was Todd.

"Soooo," he said with puppy dog eyes and a pouty lip already forming on his face. "I know this is your birthday celebration, but how would you feel about doing your oldest bestest friend a favor? I was thinking we could cut out of here early and take this party back to your dad's place. Maybe our *friends* could just crash there for the night."

"Oh ummm," I hesitated, unsure if it was a good idea to have a sleepover with my sexy, totally off limits friend.

"I'm cool with it if you are," Jenny chimed in, sounding strangely sober compared to just a moment ago.

I shrugged my shoulders and followed the three of them out of the bar where we called for a ride back to my dad's house. As soon as we were at the house, Ryan and Todd gave us both a hug and then retreated to the guest room.

"Someone's getting lucky tonight," I said with a laugh as I poured two big glasses of water for us.

"I think Ryan really likes Todd," Jenny said as she

grabbed one of the glasses and headed toward the couch.

"Oh yeah? What makes you say that?" I asked as I took the spot next to her.

"He hasn't stopped talking about him since you guys arrived here," Jenny explained with a laugh.

"That's good, because Todd hasn't stopped talking about Ryan since I first showed him a picture and told him about his non profit."

"Ryan is a really good guy. I'm not sure if this was just a fling or what since they live on opposite coasts, but I know that Ryan wouldn't do anything to hurt Todd. He doesn't have a mean bone in his body," Jenny informed me sincerely.

"That's good because Todd hasn't always had it the easiest since coming out. More of his problems were in high school, but after what he's been through, he deserves to be happy."

A look of sadness crossed Jenny's face as she stared down at the ground. "Yeah, I know how that is," she said as she continued to avoid looking at me.

I figured this was one of those things that Jenny didn't want to talk about, but felt so helpless in that moment. All I wanted was to make her feel better.

I lifted her chin so she was forced to look in my eyes.

"You know you can talk to me about anything. I'll always be here to listen."

A small smile finally crossed Jenny's face. "I know and I appreciate that. And I just want you to know that I'm not trying to keep secrets from you. There are just certain things that are too hard for me to talk about." She took a deep breath before adding, "Enough sadness though. Let's talk about something happier. What are your goals for your 25th year of life, aside from continuing to be a complete lady killer?"

I thought about the question sincerely for a minute, not having given much thought to it. "I guess I'd like to travel more, expand my business, and spend more time volunteering and giving back to charity. I'd also like to learn more about the mysterious Jenny Hanson. That is if you'll let me. What about you?"

Jenny placed a finger over her dimple as she thought about the question. I swear every move this girl made was a form of calculated flirtation. "I'd obviously like to move up in my company if that's at all possible and spend more time with friends and family, which would include the pretty girl sitting right in front of me."

"Would it be completely pathetic of me to admit that I'm really going to miss you?" I asked with a sigh.

"No, because I'm going to miss you too. At least since you scored yourself a wedding invite, we'll get to see each other again in four months."

Four months. That seemed like an eternity when it came to Jenny, which was silly since I hadn't even known her a year at this point.

We spent the next few hours talking about friends and family and trips that we took as kids. After awhile, I noticed that Jenny could barely keep her eyes open.

"We should get to bed," I announced while eyeing up the clock that now read 3:30am. "I have to head to the airport in just a few hours. You can sleep in my room. I'll take the couch."

I directed Jenny to my bedroom, gave her a shirt and shorts of mine to wear to bed, and tucked her in.

"You sure know how to treat a lady," Jenny said while smiling up at me from the bed. "You know. It is a big bed and probably much more comfy than the couch. You could always join me if you wanted to."

I saw a look of doubt cross Jenny's face as soon as the words were out of her mouth. As excited as the idea of sharing a bed with Jenny made me, I knew that was the exact reason that I couldn't.

"I don't think I've ever joined a girl in bed and kept

things completely friendly. If you were Todd, instead of a gorgeous girl who I happen to have a lot of chemistry with, this would be a different story. But you're not. So I think I'll stick to my plan of sleeping on the couch."

I was awoken just a few hours later to the sound of my alarm. I stood up from my dad's couch and knocked on both bedroom doors as a wake up call. Within an hour, Todd and I had said our goodbyes and were on our way to the airport. I noticed that Todd was quiet on most of the ride, but didn't want to push him to talk before he was ready.

Once we had boarded the plane, I figured I had given him enough time to wallow in self pity or self reflect or do whatever it was he was doing.

I put a hand on his knee and squeezed. "Talk to me buddy. What's up with you and Ryan? Did you guys talk at all about what this past week meant? You were pretty much inseparable."

For the first time since leaving, a smile came onto Todd's face. "Rory. Ryan is perfect. He's good looking, sweet, and so sincere. He's also very talented in other ways, if you catch my drift."

"Ok," I said through a fake gag. "Moving on. Do you think you guys will keep in touch once we're back home?"

"It's more than that Rory. We didn't put a label on it

because it's so early, but at this point, neither of us is interested in seeing anyone else. We're going to see how the distance thing goes, but if we can make it through until next summer, I honestly think I might move to California."

His words almost made me choke on my drink.

"Whoa. Slow down there. Are you sure *you're* not the lesbian? Aren't gay guys supposed to hook up and move on?"

"Clearly that's your role in this friendship," he jabbed at me. "Seriously though Rory, when you know you know. And I really think Ryan could be special."

I was happy to hear him say special instead of *the one* because this was already a bit too much for me to handle. Don't get me wrong, I was happy for him. I just worried that he was setting himself up to get hurt. I told him my concerns and he said that he appreciated it, but he was willing to risk it.

I found my mind drifting to Jenny and how the words *when you know you know* made me immediately think of her. But what did that mean? What did I know? That she was going to always be an important part of my life or was there something more to it? I tried to push those thoughts away. Jenny was my friend, one of the best friends I could ask for, and that's all I needed her to be. Now I just had to figure out how to get through the next four months without seeing her. I figured I might as well enjoy myself and of course I had a few ideas on how to do that.

Chapter 8

As I boarded the plane to Miami, I reflected on the past four months and was happy about the fact that they had surprisingly flown by. I thought about my dinner with Todd the night before when he updated me on how things were going with Ryan - *just perfectly* he had said with a sigh - and how he had again made fun of me for my relationship with Jenny. He had pointed out that while I still had a "back to school" girlfriend (which, in his words, is a girl that I date so I can take her to local school district activities and sporting events that my company sponsors), I had skipped out on a "holiday girlfriend" this year. I argued with him that the reason I didn't date anyone over the holidays was because I was spending time with my mom and that was the truth. I stayed with my mom back in my childhood home from Thanksgiving all the way through christmas and had left early this morning to drive to the airport.

Just a few hours later, I landed in Miami, got my luggage, and headed to the rental car area. I had told Jenny that I would rent a car so I could drive us to and from the airport and anywhere else we might want to go. Her flight was scheduled to land about a half hour after mine, so by the time I got the car and pulled it up to the pick up area, Jenny was waiting outside with her luggage. I immediately hopped out of the car and wrapped her in a big hug, taking in her scent as I held her close. As weird as it might sound, I think I missed her smell more than anything when we were apart.

"It's so good to see you finally," I said as we pulled apart.

Jenny took my face in her hands. "You're telling me. FaceTime and Skype just don't do this pretty face justice."

She looked past me at the rental, which was a red mustang convertible, and shook her head. "Seriously? You had to get the showy car?"

I shrugged my shoulders. "When in Miami, am I right? Plus, when you are driving around a girl who is this ridiculously pretty, you need a nice car to match."

Jenny hopped over the door into the passenger seat and ran her hand along the dashboard. "Still. I hope you didn't pay a lot of extra for this," she said sincerely. "I already feel guilty enough that you're paying for the hotel room for the week."

I climbed into the car and put my hand on top of Jenny's, while smiling over at her. "I told you not to worry about it, ok? I know money is tight living in LA."

"That actually reminds me. I have news to share with you," Jenny said excitedly. "I just found out on Monday, but wanted to wait until we were together to tell you. I'm getting promoted to junior producer in January. Before you get too excited, the title sounds much more fancy than it actually is. Pretty much I get to work on movie sets and be the main producer's bitch. But I'm getting a pay raise and it will give me more hands on experience. Plus, they asked me to start thinking about possible screenplay or documentary ideas. It's not likely that they would actually move forward with any of my ideas at this point, but it's still exciting!"

It was exciting and watching the way Jenny's face lit up when she talked about it was easily one of my favorite things in the world.

I put my hand on her knee and smiled over at her. "I'm so proud of you," I said sincerely and I truly was. This girl amazed me more and more each time we were together.

The rest of the drive was spent enjoying the warm Miami breeze and listening to music. When we arrived at the hotel, I was stunned by the view. I had stayed a lot of nice places throughout my travels, but this was probably the nicest. The beachfront hotel was not just massive, but also luxurious. It was no wonder I had dropped a lot of money for us to stay there. It was also no surprise that the guest list for the wedding was so small. I believe Jenny told me that there would be 50 people attending and at least half of them were family. We made our way to the front desk, where a very pretty concierge, who must have been just a few years older than us, checked us in.

I noticed the way her eyes lingered on both Jenny and I as she smiled at us from behind the counter. Instinctively, I put my hand on Jenny's shoulder, although I'm not quite sure why I did.

"Alright," she said, while clearing her throat. "It looks like we have the king suite reserved for you for six nights."

I felt my body warming up when I heard the mention of a king size bed. That couldn't have been what I had reserved, unless I did it out of habit.

"Umm actually," I mumbled as I stumbled over my words, "I believe.. I think.. I actually reserved the room with two queen beds."

I cringed as the words came out, hoping Jenny didn't realize how overwhelmed I was at the thought of us sharing a bed.

"Oh yeah. That's right," the concierge corrected. "I'm very sorry. I read that wrong." She stared at my hand for a split second then added, "We do have an upgrade available for a king suite if you'd like it. No extra charge."

"Oh um.. no thank you. Two beds are good for us. Just friends and all, so space is good." What was up with this rambling? It was ridiculous how much of a mess I became around Jenny.

The rest of the check in process thankfully went by quickly, without me sticking my foot in my mouth anymore than I already had. When Jenny left to get a luggage cart, the concierge whose name I now learned was Vanessa, leaned in close to me.

"I'm really sorry about earlier," Vanessa confessed. "I didn't mean to assume that you guys are gay. I swear sometimes my gaydar runs wild. You know, wishful thinking and all."

I smiled back at her, thinking how cute she looked now that she was the one who was flustered.

"You have nothing to worry about," I said with a wink. "Your gaydar was not wrong. We are both very gay. We are also very much just friends."

Vanessa's face lit up at these words. "Well, in that case," she said as she pulled out a business card and scribbled what I had to assume was her cell phone number on the back. "Feel free to get ahold of me if you want a personal tour of Miami or, you know, if you'd just like to get a drink sometime."

"Thanks Vanessa," I said while maintaining drawn out eye contact. "I just might take you up on that offer."

I started to walk away, then something inside told me to turn back around. I'm not sure which part of me that was, but I can definitely tell you which part it wasn't.

"Actually, I have to be honest. I'm probably not going to call. I just wanted to tell you that now because I don't want you to think it has anything to do with you. You're beautiful and I would have to assume that we would have an amazing time together, but the thing is, I'm here with someone else. And while we truly are just friends, I still plan on devoting all of my time to her this week. But if you don't mind, I think I'll go ahead and keep your number and if I happen to be in Miami again sometime, I'll be sure to get ahold of you."

I was happy when a genuine smile formed on Vanessa's lips. "Sounds good. But don't worry, I won't hold my breath on that. You have fun with your *friend*."

I couldn't help but notice the change in her tone as she said the word friend and raised both eyebrows as it left her mouth, but I chose to ignore it.

When I got over to Jenny, she stared at the card in my hand, but didn't say anything. Since she wasn't going to acknowledge it, I decided it was for the best if I didn't either. I slipped it into my back pocket and we made our way to our hotel room.

As soon as we were in the room, I threw myself onto

my bed. "So, what's the plan the rest of the day?" I asked Jenny.

"There's nothing official planned until tomorrow when we have the bachelorette party. Sunday and Monday are also pretty open aside from the rehearsal dinner. I figured those days would be perfect to get a little more color on that northeast skin of yours."

I stuck my tongue out at Jenny as I threw a pillow at her. "Very funny. Are you sure it's cool if I go to the bachelorette party? I don't want to intrude."

"Of course it's cool," Jenny reassured me. "Unless of course you didn't want to go, you know, if you had something you'd rather do."

Even though she was smiling, I noticed a hint of annoyance in Jenny's voice as she said the last part. I wondered if it had anything to do with the fact that I had gotten Vanessa's number. Although, I'm not sure why that would bother her. Except I knew that it would have bothered me if it was reversed, even if it shouldn't have.

"There's nothing I'd rather do," I said with a smile. "I'm never going to turn down extra time with you. I just don't want to overstep my boundaries since this week is about Allison and Bret."

A sincere smile returned to Jenny's face. "You're not

overstepping any boundaries. Allison specifically told me that she wants you there."

"Then I'm definitely in." I looked at the clock and saw that it was already past 6. "Listen. Not to sound like a total loser, but I'm super tired from traveling. Would you have any interest in ordering room service and renting a movie?"

Jenny agreed and we spent the rest of the night eating, watching movies, and catching up.

After breakfast the next day, we got ready and headed down to the beach. The plan was to day drink on the beach and go out for dinner and drinks later that night. When we got down to the beach, the rest of the bridal party was already there. It was comprised of Allison's younger sister, her cousin, and two friends from college that I found out had lived with Allison and Jenny for their third and fourth years of college.

After being formally introduced, we started stripping down into our bikinis. As I caught Jenny taking off her shirt out of the corner of my eye it occurred to me that this was the first time I was seeing her in a bathing suit. I couldn't resist turning toward her to get a better look and, my God, did that girl know how to rock a bikini. The bikini hung just right on her flat stomach and perfect chest and butt.

As I ran my eyes up and down her body, Jenny turned toward me. She bent her head to bring her eyes down to mine.

"My eyes are up here," she said with a cocky smirk, before adding, "And you might want to pick your jaw up off the ground."

I could feel my face turning red, but Jenny just laughed and put a hand on my shoulder.

She then leaned in close to whisper in my ear. "You need to take some lessons from me. I know how to drool over a pretty girl in a bikini without being caught. Unless, of course, you noticed."

I took a deep breath as she leaned back and winked at me, trying to gain my composure back. Before I could think of what to say, Jenny grabbed sunscreen out of her bag and held it up.

"I'll get your back if you get mine?" She asked.

I nodded then sat down on the sand behind her and poured sunscreen into my hands. As I spread the sunscreen over Jenny's back, I couldn't help but think about how nice it was to feel her skin under my hands. I thought there was no sweeter torture than this until we switched spots and she started applying it on my back. Every spot she touched felt like it was on fire. I sighed to myself and closed my eyes, allowing myself to enjoy this feeling.

I was interrupted by someone speaking beside me. It was Allison's cousin, Barbara. "You two are so cute together. How long have you been dating?"

It took me a moment to realize she was talking to Jenny and I. I hesitated, unsure what to say, and Jenny dropped her hands from my back down to her sides. Allison reached over and put her hands over Jenny's ears.

"Shhh Barb. We don't say the word date in front of Jenny. It gives her hives," she joked. She then leaned closer to Barbara and not-so-quietly whispered, "Aren't they adorable though?"

"Rory and I are just friends. We met at a wedding about a year ago," Jenny finally said, smiling over at me.

"A year and two months to be exact," I added.

Allison and her cousin shared a knowing look, but didn't say anything else and the rest of the day luckily went by without any awkward encounters.

When it was time to finally go out, most of the girls had a pretty strong buzz going. I decided I wasn't going to drink anything because I wanted to be able to help out if anyone became too drunk. Jenny had a few drinks, but had also decided to stay in the right frame of mind. That was not the case with Allison's sister, Erin, who had just turned 21 a few weeks earlier and was excited that one of her first times legally drinking was being spent in Miami beach. Only an hour into our time at the first bar, she was already swaying and slurring her words.

"I'm here boyssssss," she shouted as she twirled herself in a circle and just barely kept her footing.

Allison, who was also pretty toasted glared at her sister. "I swear if you ruin this night, I am going to kill you. You need to grow the hell up."

Erin just smiled, unaware of just how serious her sister was. "I don't need to grow up. I'm just going to drink more drinks and meet some boys. I'm also going to…" She stopped suddenly and stared at the ceiling, then turned toward the group with a panicked look in her eyes. "I'm also going to be sick."

I grabbed ahold of her arms to steady her and turned toward Allison, who looked like she was either going to blow her top or start to cry. "I'm going to walk your sister outside to get some fresh air. Don't worry. I can handle it. You just have a good time."

Before leaving, I ordered another round of shots for the group, after extensively reassuring the bartender that Erin, who was now resting her head on my shoulder, wouldn't be getting one of them. We then carefully made our way out of the bar and onto the street. We walked for awhile until we ended up on the beach.

Erin took a deep breath. "I think I'm feeling better," she slurred. "We can go back to the bar now. The boyssss are waiting."

Before I could respond, her face turned a different shade and she bent over and started puking. I decided it was for the best if I got her back to the hotel before she got arrested for public intoxication. I had to imagine that's not what Allison's parents would want to deal with on top of making sure their other daughter's wedding went smoothly.

As we started walking toward the hotel, I pulled out my phone and sent a text to Jenny, figuring she wouldn't be able to hear much in the bar. A minute later, she was calling me.

"Do you need me to meet you guys back there?" she asked, with a hint of concern in her voice.

"Of course not," I reassured her. "This is your best friend's bachelorette party. You should be there. I'll make sure Erin is ok. It's nothing water and tylenol can't fix."

"Ok.." she said hesitantly. "If you insist. Thank you so much for doing this Rory. You really didn't have to."

"I know. I want to." And I really did. Honestly, I would do anything for Jenny and the people she cares about.

That's how much she meant to me.

When we got back to the hotel, I asked Erin what room she was staying in and her eyes went wide. "I'm sharing a room with my parents. I can't go back there. They'll kill me."

I just laughed and shook my head. "You're ok kid. We'll go back to my hotel room."

As soon as we were in the room, Erin started puking again. Luckily, she was able to make it to the toilet this time. I grabbed a hair tie and pulled her hair back as she continued to hug the toilet. She stayed this way for a few more minutes before lifting her head to look at me.

"I think I'm really done this time," she announced.

I gave her another few minutes just to be on the safe side then asked if she was able to change on her own. She gave me a thumbs up so I tossed her a pair of shorts and a T-shirt of mine, then shut the door to the bathroom. A minute later Erin emerged and laid down in my bed.

I pointed to the bottle of water and Tylenol I had sat on the nightstand for her. "Take that medicine and make sure you drink the whole bottle of water before passing out."

Erin quickly drank the water as I grabbed a trash can and sat it by her bed. "Just Incase," I said with a wink.

Before I could turn away, Erin grabbed my hand.

"You're so nice. And you're so so pretty. Are you suuuuuure Jenny isn't your girlfriend?"

I laughed and squeezed her hand. "Yes. I'm sure."

"But why not?" She pressed. "Jenny is terrific."

I sighed. "You're right about that. Jenny is the most fantastic person I've ever met. She's truly special. But neither of us is into relationships, so we're strictly friends."

"Have you guys at least had some hot sex?"

I shook my head at her question, knowing she wouldn't be this nosy if she was sober. "No we haven't."

Erin looked sincerely shocked. "But why not? Are you not sexually attracted to Jenny?"

I laughed again. "I think I would have to be either blind or straight to not be sexually attracted to Jenny."

"Then what are you waiting for? This is your chance. You should totally get it in this trip." Erin winked after her statement.

"I would never do that," I said seriously. "I respect Jenny way too much for that. I wouldn't ever want to make her feel like just another hook up. She's so much more than that."

Erin shut her eyes and I thought she had passed out until she started talking again a few minutes later. "It's too bad Jenny can't be your exception. You know, that person that makes you change your thoughts on relationships. Jenny has been like a big sister to me since her and Allison got close in high school. She deserves to have someone amazing like you. She deserves so much happiness, especially after all the crap that she went through."

I wanted to push Erin to elaborate on what she was sayings. What was all the crap Jenny had gone through? Was that the reason she was so against relationships? Before I could ask anything, I heard a snore come from Erin's direction. I sighed. It was probably for the best anyway. Jenny should be the one to tell me about her past, not anyone else.

As if she knew I was talking about her, Jenny walked through the door just at that moment. She looked over at my bed that was holding a now snoring Erin.

"How is she?" She asked.

"She's fine. She's officially emptied out all of the contents of her stomach. She might have a bit of a headache tomorrow, but hopefully that's as bad as it gets." I walked over to give Jenny a hug then added, "How was the rest of your night?"

"It was good. We had a lot of fun and Allison didn't get hung up on her sister thanks to you. Although it did end with the other half of this sister duo puking all over the bathroom of her hotel room."

I cringed. "Oh yuck. That's not going to be fun to wake up to tomorrow."

"The hangover might not be, but the bathroom is nice and clean thanks to yours truly," Jenny informed me with a cocky grin.

"Well, aren't you just the #1 bachelorette party mom there is?" I joked as I pulled myself closer to Jenny.

"I'd say I'm number two," she said smiling at me. "You beat me tonight. But don't get to stuck on it. I'm still the number one wedding attendee."

"So you say," I quipped, returning her cocky grin. "But were you the one who was invited to a wedding the first time she met the bride and groom? Oh wait. No. That was me."

Jenny raised an eyebrow at me as if to say *two can play at this game.* "Have you forgotten about my DJ invite?"

Shoot. She had me there. "Touché. We'll call it a draw for now. But it won't stay that way for long."

Jenny laughed then let out a long yawn before looking between her empty bed and my bed that Erin was currently occupying.

"I'll just sleep on the couch," I said, reading her thoughts.

"Nonsense. You've done enough tonight. You deserve to get a good night's sleep. You take my bed and I'll bunk with drunkie over here. It wouldn't be the first time we squeezed into a bed together and most of the time we have a third person joining us."

I quirked my mouth into a half smile. "You know, if I didn't understand the context of that statement, I'd think you were quite the dirty bird. But then again, I have a feeling you have uttered a phrase similar to that under different circumstances."

"Wouldn't you like to know?" Jenny asked while raising a seductive eyebrow at me. "You can fantasize about that while sleeping in my bed tonight."

I laughed as I crawled into bed, but the truth was, as I laid there surrounded by Jenny's scent, I was fantasizing about her. It wasn't the type of fantasy I would ever expect to have though. I was fantasizing about what it would feel like to have her cuddled up beside me in bed. I'm not going to lie, I loved sharing a good cuddle session with whatever girl I was dating, but cuddling had never made me feel as hot and bothered as just the thought of cuddling with Jenny. I let her scent overtake me and smiled as I drifted off to sleep.

The days leading up to the wedding were pretty relaxing and the rehearsal dinner had run very smoothly. On

New Year's Eve, which was the day of the wedding, I woke up early to set out on a mission. Jenny had spent the previous night with Allison and the other bridesmaids. They had asked me to also stay in the suite with them, but I declined as I didn't want to intrude on their time. I quickly got dressed and went out to find a good donut shop and a grocery store.

Two hours later, I dropped off donuts and mimosas in the girls' suite and donuts and beer in the boys' suite. I also informed both groups that I had sandwiches being delivered mid afternoon. I always heard it was important to make sure the bride and groom ate on their wedding day and thought it was especially important since their ceremony didn't start until 6:00 so dinner wouldn't be until after 8. I spent most of the day hanging out with the guys since they were much more relaxed, but did stop by the girl's room every so often so I could check if Jenny needed anything.

When the time for the wedding came around, I headed down to the beach where the ceremony spot had been set up and took a seat in the back. Since the sun had already started to set, there were a bunch of pretty lights set up surrounding the area. I thought about how much money Allison's parents must have spent on this wedding and then found my mind wandering to what kind of wedding I would want, that is if I was ever going to have one. I figured I would want my wedding to be as me (and of course my wife) as possible. While money would be no object, I wasn't interested in anything lavish. Correction, I wasn't interested in anything at all. Why was my mind even going there?

My thoughts were interrupted by the processional music beginning. When Jenny walked down the aisle, I felt my heart skip a beat just like the first time I had met her. She looked exquisite. The bridesmaids dresses were a green color that reminded me of the one she wore to our cousins' wedding and she had her hair done up in a loose bun with just a few pieces hanging out. I was so distracted watching Jenny that I almost missed Allison walking down the aisle. The ceremony went by in a flash and I honestly couldn't tell you anything that happened because I couldn't take my eyes off of Jenny.

I waited at the end of the beach for the wedding party to get pictures and smiled at Jenny as she walked over toward me. When she was close, I took her hand and twirled her in a circle.

"I can't lie Miss Hanson. You look absolutely breathtaking," I told Jenny sincerely.

"You don't look so bad yourself Miss Montgomery," Jenny said with a wink.

We walked back to the hotel where the reception was

being held and helped ourselves to some drinks and hors d'oeuvres, then found our table where Jenny introduced me to two more of her friends from college. She then slipped away to join the rest of the wedding party before introductions started.

"So, how long have you and Jenny been dating?" The one girl, whose name I had just learned was Karen, asked. She was a short petite blonde which was a funny contrast to her boyfriend, Paul, who looked like he was some sort of body builder.

I smiled at her question but wondered if people would ever stop assuming that Jenny and I were together. "We're not dating," I informed her. "We're just good friends."

Her other friend, Lisa, leaned closer to us. "That makes more sense. I was going to ask you your secret. You know, how you managed to tame her. I don't think that girl will ever be tamed."

Her husband, Tom, laughed beside her. "I still remember when I met her, the first time I visited this one at school. She was such a fireball and so confident. I felt like everyone on campus already knew her."

"That's because they all wanted to date her," Karen chimed in. "Even all of the guys were trying to get with her, even though she was very outspoken about the fact that she was gay."

"You can't blame them for thinking they had a chance though. That girl would flirt with anyone and everyone," Lisa added and everyone nodded in agreement.

"So, Rory, don't take this the wrong way but are you straight or gay?" Paul asked.

Karen rolled her eyes at her boyfriend and slapped him in the arm. He smiled and sheepishly raised his hands in apology.

I smiled so Karen and Paul would know that I wasn't offended by the question. "Ha. It's a logical question. No worries. I'm gay."

Lisa let out a low whistle. "Maybe you did tame her. I don't think Jenny has ever been just friends with another lesbian. She never even joined our college's gay club because she said it would be a conflict of interest or something like that. But we all knew that meant that she had hooked up with most of the girls who attended the meetings."

Karen laughed and put a hand on my shoulder. "Oh girl. We have so many Jenny stories to share with you before this night is over."

Before she could say anything else, the DJ announced that the wedding party introductions were about to start. I was happy about this interruption. For some reason, I had no interest in hearing about Jenny's wild college days.

After the introductions and first dance were over, both Jenny and Allison made their way over to our table. I greeted them and told Allison how beautiful she looked and how nice the ceremony was.

"Thank you," she said. "I see that you had the chance to meet the rest of the UCLA crew."

"Yes. They are all great," I said while smiling at the group. Then I did a quick sweep around the room to see if there was anyone else who seemed to be around our age. "Do you guys have any high school friends here? I'd love to meet them too."

Jenny's face turned sour as she stared at the ground and mumbled a quick "No."

Allison smiled through gritted teeth and put a hand on Jenny's shoulder. "We don't talk to any of those people anymore. Girls from our high school are huge bitches."

"Oh," I said quickly, putting a hand on Jenny's arm and bending to try to catch her eyes. "Well screw them. You guys are way too good for people like that."

"Preach it girl," Allison said while raising a fist for me to bump.

At this point, Jenny finally allowed her eyes to make contact with mine and a smile slowly spread across her face.

"Yeah. There's no room for people like that in my life. Especially when I have a pretty girl like you to give all of my attention to."

And just like that she was back - the Jenny I had grown to know and...appreciate a lot. This was the Jenny that her college friends seemed to know as well. So, what was this other side of Jenny? It seemed to be a side that she had left in high school. It was a side that was timid and unsure and vulnerable. As much as I liked the cool and confident side of Jenny, I wanted to get to know this side as well. I was desperate to know every part of her. But in just two days, we would be back on opposite sides of the country and I found myself wishing more and more that this wasn't the case. More than anything, I wanted the chance to spend more time with her.

Chapter 9

I stepped into the driver's side of the big moving truck and smiled over at Todd. "California here we come," I sang as I rolled the windows down and waved goodbye to our hometown.

"I can't believe we're actually doing this right now," Todd said with excitement pouring from his voice.

"It is pretty crazy," I agreed. "Moving across the country is a huge step."

"I'm just so excited," he practically screamed. The smile left his face as he gave me a serious look. "But how are you feeling?"

"I'm super excited for you as well, not to mention extremely jealous. You're going to be living in my favorite place in the whole world. But I'm also very sad. I know we haven't lived in the same place for awhile now, but a two hour drive was much easier than a five hour plane ride. I'm not going to lie, it's going to be hard not seeing you as much. We've been through everything together."

Todd stared at me and, for a moment, I thought he might start to cry. Instead, he reached out and grabbed my hand. "I'm going to miss you like crazy too. It feels weird making such a big move without you."

"But it's the right move," I said sincerely, wanting to reassure him.

And I truly felt that way. Todd and Ryan had been dating just shy of a year at this point and were madly in love. At first, I wondered how it was possible to develop feelings like that when they weren't physically in each others presence. In the 11 months they were together so far, they had each made one trip to see the other person so the majority of their time was spent texting and Skyping. When Todd told me he was going to be moving to LA and moving in with Ryan, he explained that the distance was exactly why they had gotten so close. Since their time wasn't spent doing activities together, they talked and learned everything about each other. It made sense. I felt closer to Jenny than anyone else in my life, with the exception of maybe my mom and Todd.

Todd smiled. "It still doesn't feel right to move across the country without you. I really thought all of my begging and pleading would be enough to convince my oldest, bestest friend to move to her favorite place in the world with me. It's not even like *you* would have to give up your job to go."

I squeezed Todd's hand. "I'm sure you'll find a teaching job in no time," I reassured him.

I knew that was the one factor that made him question

the move. He was still living in our small hometown at his childhood home, so he was more than happy to leave that. He just wondered if he should be leaving a stable job without having another one in place. Luckily, Ryan had promised to let him work at his non profit while he looked for a full time teaching position. Ryan would have promised anything to get Todd to move out with him and I was happy that he had found someone like that.

"I'm going to try this one more time," Todd said, interrupting my thoughts. "Will you pretty pretty please with cherries on top just consider moving to California?" He jutted out his lip, showing the most pathetic puppy dog face.

"You know I can't do that," I said seriously. "I've already told you a thousand times why I'm not going to."

Todd sighed. "I know and I respect your reasoning. I don't agree with it, but I respect it. I'm just asking you to consider taking a lesson from me though. Stop overthinking it and just do it."

"It's different for you. You're moving so you can be with the love of your life."

A sly grin came onto Todd's face. "I mean you would be moving to be with the love of your life as well."

I laughed and rolled my eyes at him. "Don't give yourself so much credit. I love you to pieces, but not in that way."

"Oh stop. You and I both know that I'm not talking about myself. How many girls have you dated since the last time you saw Jenny?" The smile on his face grew wider as he spoke.

"I don't know Todd. Maybe two or three. This game is getting old, you know. You act like I've gone completely celibate."

"That practically is celibate for you," Todd said with a laugh. "Plus, I don't even believe you. You never talk to me about girls anymore."

I shot Todd a stern look and warned him to drop the subject. Luckily for me, he did. We spent the next five days of our road trip stopping in different locations to rest and sight see and never again spoke of me moving to California or my non-existent love life.

When we got to LA, our first stop was at Jenny and Ryan's current apartment so we could add Ryan's belongings to the moving truck. Since the apartment was located so close to her job and she now had the money to afford it on her own, Jenny had decided to transfer the lease to her name. Ryan and Todd were renting an apartment about a mile from her.

When we walked inside, I realized it was my first

time seeing the apartment in person. It was definitely small, but also cute. I had to imagine it would be even cuter once Jenny had full reign over the decorations. The two twin beds that had adorned the bedroom before had already been replaced by a queen size bed with cute pink and blue flowers on the white comforter.

After saying hello, we quickly got to work moving the little furniture that Ryan was taking with him out of the apartment. I was impressed by how strong Jenny was as we moved from her apartment and into Ryan and Todd's new one. When everything was unloaded, I threw myself onto one of the couches that Ryan had gotten delivered earlier in the week and Jenny sat down beside me.

"Hi," I said smiling over at her, realizing we hadn't had much of a chance to talk yet.

"Why hello there," Jenny said as she leaned closer to me. "There's been something I've been meaning to do all day."

My breath hitched as I tried to wrap my head around what she was talking about. She reached her hand out and squeezed my bicep.

"Who knew you were hiding such big muscles under those arms of yours?" Jenny winked as she said the words and kept her hand on my arm.

I gave her a half smile and purposely flexed my arm, before reaching out to grab hers. "Funny. I was actually thinking the same thing about you."

I was about to get lost in Jenny's eyes when I heard laughter coming from behind us.

"So sorry to interrupt," Todd joked, while Ryan stood beside him snickering.

I glared at them both and Ryan cleared his throat. "We were thinking we could set up the tv, order some pizza, and spend the night watching movies. What do you guys think?"

I quickly agreed. Nothing sounded better than snuggling close to Jenny while watching movies, so that's what we did.

I was awoken the next day to the sound of my phone ringing. I blinked at it a few times when I saw my dad's name appear on the screen. He never called me out of the blue.

"Dad? Is everything ok?" I asked immediately, skipping hellos.

"Everything is fine baby girl. Are you in LA right now? I saw you posted something on Facebook about it."

Guilt coursed through me, even though I told myself I should never feel guilty about anything when it came to my dad. "Yeah I am. Sorry I didn't tell you dad. I just came to help Todd move. I actually leave tomorrow."

"That's ok," he spoke. I realized his voice sounded chipper than usual. "Any chance I could see you today? Maybe we could do dinner? You can bring your friends. I know you don't have much time with them."

I wanted to ask who this man on the phone was and what he did with my dad, but decided to just go along with it.

That night, Jenny, Ryan, Todd, and I met my dad and Monica at a cute little Italian restaurant near the Hollywood walk of fame. Both my dad and Monica had goofy grins on their faces as they greeted us.

Monica looked at my dad with an excited shimmer in her eyes. "Can we tell them now?"

"Well, it looks like we're not wasting any time," my dad chuckled. "Sure. Go ahead."

Monica immediately lifted her hand towards us, showing off the large, shiny engagement ring that decorated her ring finger.

"We're engaged," my dad shouted. "I just popped the question a few days ago and was trying to think of the right time to tell you, then I saw that you were in the area and knew I couldn't miss the chance to tell you in person."

I hesitated for a moment and all eyes fell on me. I

reached out my hand and patted my dad on the shoulder. "That's great Dad. I'm really happy for you guys."

Upon hearing this, all of my friends joined in, telling my dad and Monica how excited they were and gushing over Monica's ring. Oh yeah. These were definitely some good friends.

We spent most of the dinner talking about the proposal and the wedding that they were most likely going to do next summer. After we were done eating, my dad asked if he could talk to me outside alone. I thought it was a bit strange and out of character for him, but I agreed anyway.

We stood outside awkwardly for a few minutes before my dad started to talk. It always seemed weird to me that at times my dad felt like a complete stranger and others he felt like one of my best friends. Right now he definitely was falling closer to the stranger side.

"So," he said hesitantly, running a hand through his hair. "I was wondering if you would be my... girl of honor.. or umm best girl.. or whatever they call it these days. We're not doing a wedding party. We're way too old for that sort of thing, but Monica and I both agreed that we want you to stand up front with us during the ceremony."

"Of course I will Dad," I choked out, trying to hold back tears. I'm not sure why he was still able to have this effect on me, but he was my dad, no matter how he acted most of the time.

A relieved look entered his face. "That's great. I'm so happy to hear it. I was also wondering if you wanted to maybe help us plan it. Monica is going to take care of the decorating, but I thought you might want to help with a venue and all of the fun parts like music, food, photography, and what not. You don't have to though. I know I don't deserve it. I just thought it might be something fun for us to do together. I'd be happy to pay for any flights you would take to come here."

I took a deep breath. This was all a lot to take in. The thought of helping my dad plan his wedding did seem exciting to me, but I wasn't ready to commit yet.

"Could I think about it?" I asked.

"Of course you can sweetheart. Take your time."

Truthfully, I knew the only time I needed was the time it would take for me to talk to one certain person.

Chapter 10

Just a week into being home from California, I drove back to my hometown to visit my mom. She didn't think anything of it when I asked to come visit because I normally tried to visit her at least once a month, if not more. But I was nervous because I knew this time was different. I was going with the mission to talk to her about my dad's wedding. I had a feeling she didn't know anything about it since the two of them had cut off all communication after he moved out.

I had planned to wait a few days to say anything, but the first night we were having dinner together my mom caught on.

"Why are you so quiet?" She pressed. "And please don't try to lie. I know you and I know when you are trying to hide something from me."

I knew she was right. My mom had practically come out for me. She could read me like a book.

"Dad's getting married," I blurted out.

"That's nice," she said nonchalantly. "Are you ok with that?"

"I mean...I don't know. I guess...I mean. Yeah?" I knew my answer didn't really make any sense, but I didn't want to hurt my mom's feeling by saying the wrong thing.

My mom looked concerned. "What are you unsure of? Do you not like his fiancé? Was she mean to you?" A bit of anger flashed into her voice as she asked that last question.

"No. No. She wasn't mean to me. She's actually really nice and funny." I quickly added, "But you're better of course. She could never be as great as you."

My mom laughed a loud hardy laugh. "Oh honey, you're worried about me, aren't you?"

I just nodded in response and my mom pulled me into a hug. "Oh Ror. You don't have to worry about me. Your dad and I have been over for years and I know you saw a lot of ugliness between us, but I really do want him to be happy."

I let out a breath of relief. "There is one more thing," I informed my mom. "Dad asked me to help him plan the wedding."

"That's nice. What did you tell him?"

"I told him I would think about it. I wanted to talk to you first."

My mom smiled at me. "Well, do you want to do it?"

"I think I do," I admitted. "No actually, I definitely do. I know I probably shouldn't want to. I don't owe him anything, but it feels good that he asked me."

"Then you should do it," my mom said sincerely. "I think this will be good for you guys. I've always felt bad that you didn't have a close relationship with your dad. I worried it was my fault, like somehow I was holding you back."

I shook my head gesturing that it wasn't. My mom couldn't control how my dad acted. But it was settled. I was going to do this.

Before I called my dad to tell him, I dialed Jenny's number.

When she picked up, I didn't even bother saying hello and just cut to the chase. "How do you feel about helping me plan a wedding?"

The next year was insane. My time was spent traveling back and forth between Pennsylvania and California, as well as anywhere else that I needed to travel for work. Since I was spending so much time on the wedding, I felt like all of my non-wedding time was spent working.

The wedding planning was fun though. Since I had convinced Jenny to help me, we were able to spend a lot of time together. I actually saw her more than I saw my dad, but that wasn't too shocking. I knew he wasn't suddenly going to be a changed man.

We looked up venues located within an hour of LA and ended up choosing one after my dad, Monica, Jenny, and I went to see it and all fell in love. Jenny and I decided it would be more fun to have a band than a DJ at their wedding and ended up finding a 50s doo-wop band that my dad quickly became obsessed with.

When the big day arrived, I was excited to see how it all came together. My dad invited Jenny to come since she had helped with the planning. I was happy to have her there since I didn't know any of the 70 people that were attending. Apparently some of them were relatives from my dad's side of the family, but I had never even met them before so they all felt like strangers.

The ceremony was short since my dad and Monica didn't want it to have any religious aspect to it. This was another point of contention between my mom and dad. My mom's side of the family was much more religious than my dad's. My mom went to church by herself for most of my childhood until I had come to know God on my own and started to go with her. My dad refused to attend even on holidays.

The reception was fun for an event that had no one in attendance under the age of 50. The band did a good job of getting people up and dancing in the beginning of the night. The dancing started to die down about an hour into the reception, which was normally my cue to get the party started. Only this time, I didn't have the motivation. I was happy for my dad and we really had grown closer over the past year, but I still felt a little bitter to all these people who seemed to get a part of him that I never did.

I stood on the edge of the dance floor looking around when I felt a hand on my back. I turned to see Jenny standing beside me.

"Everything ok? You're not your usual wedding self tonight."

I smiled. She really did know me so well. "Yeah, I'm good. Just not in the party starting mood."

"Makes sense," Jenny said knowingly. "I happened to notice that the fence to the pool isn't very high. How do you feel about climbing it and dipping our feet?"

I agreed and we made our way out of the reception hall. When we got to the pool, the fence was higher than I expected from Jenny's explanation. She stepped onto my hands and scaled the fence like an old pro, then clung to the other side and reached her hand out to pull me up.

I raised an eyebrow at her. "I take it you've done this before?"

She raised both shoulders and winked. "A magician never reveals her secret."

We walked over to the pool and dipped our feet into the water. We sat silently for a few minutes before Jenny finally spoke.

"You look a lot like your dad when you laugh, you know."

I nodded my head. "A lot of people have told me that. Apparently, when I'm really focused on something, I look more like my mom."

"Do you think your personality is more like your mom's or your dad's?" Jenny asked and unlike most people, she seemed to sincerely want to know the answer.

"It's a pretty even split. My values are more aligned with my mom's. We both value God and our relationships with others above everything else. I have my dad's sense of adventure though. I also inherited his love for LA. I'm not going to lie, I'm pretty sad that I won't have a reason to fly here every few weeks now that the wedding is over."

Jenny laughed. "You know what? I've had to deal with Todd going on and on about how he doesn't understand why you won't just move to LA and I normally just blow him off. But he might be onto something. I know people who have lived in LA since the time they were born and they love it here, yet none of them talk about it the way you do."

"Can I make a confession?" I asked while staring up at the stars.

"Of course you can," Jenny said while placing her

hand on top of mine. "You can tell me anything Rory."

I tried to ignore the sensation I was getting from her hand on mine and took a deep breath. "Living in LA would be like a dream come true to me. Honestly, when we first visited here when I was ten years old, I decided this was where I wanted to live when I grew up. Every goal list and every dream board I made from that point forward included moving to LA."

"So what changed?"

I looked from the sky into Jenny's eyes. "My Dad moved here."

Jenny went silent for a moment and her face scrunched up like she was thinking. Then, suddenly, I saw it hit her. If this was a cartoon, the lightbulb would have turned on above your head.

"You're afraid if you move here it's like you chose your dad over your mom." I noticed that Jenny's words were more of a statement than a question. She didn't have to question it because she knew me well enough to know what I was thinking.

I nodded slowly. "I'm afraid if I come here now, it will look like I'm following my dad. I never want my mom to feel like I chose him over her. I don't want her to feel like I left her too."

Jenny stared into my eyes like she was trying to see something deep inside my soul. "I get it. I don't think your mom would truly see it that way, but I can understand where you're coming from. I wish it wasn't that way though. I'm going to be honest. I would give anything to have you close to me all of the time."

My lips parted in surprise and Jenny's eyes went wide. "I mean I would give anything to have you live close to me," she corrected, but the look on her face said she meant otherwise.

We sat staring at each other and a wave of feelings rushed through me. It was a sensation I had never experienced before and it scared the crap out of me, but I still couldn't take my eyes off of her.

I finally shook myself from her magnetic pull and removed my hand from underneath hers while I stared at my feet in the pool water.

"So, how much do you like that dress?" I asked, still unable to make eye contact with her.

Jenny chuckled. "I mean I happen to think I look nice, if that's what you're asking."

"No I already figured that part out for myself," I said, finally lightening up a bit. "I'm just asking if you think you would wear it to another wedding."

"Oh god no," Jenny said quickly. "I have a strict rule against wearing the same dress to two different weddings. Why do you ask?"

I felt a mischievous grin spread across my face as I moved my arms behind Jenny and pushed her into the pool. She flailed around as soon as she hit the water. I couldn't hold back my laughter at the sight.

"Oh you think this is funny?" She asked with a fake scowl.

Before I could respond, I felt my feet being pulled into the water and soon I was floating right beside Jenny. Now she was the one laughing hysterically. It only took a few minutes for our teeth to start chattering so I jumped out of the pool and headed over to the towel bin. There was only one towel left, so I stood unbearably close to jenny and wrapped it around both of us. The feelings I was trying to avoid quickly returned and I felt myself gulp.

That's when it hit me. I had a crush on Jenny; a real heart clenching crush. I know that should have been obvious by now with the constant attraction and almosts. But this wasn't just sexual attraction. A crush was different. A crush meant having feelings that went way beyond just wondering how it would taste to have Jenny's lips on mine. A crush meant feelings and wishes. A crush was about hopes and dreams. Attraction was fun; a crush could kill you. In that moment, I knew I had to do something. I had to stop this crush before it got any worse and hurt both of us.

Chapter 11

I sat in a booth at a small diner in LA and impatiently stared at the clock. Todd was supposed to arrive fifteen minutes earlier. Normally, this wouldn't have bothered me, but I had spent the last five months since my dad's wedding in one heck of a funk. As soon as I got back home, I threw myself back into the dating scene and it was a complete disaster. I compared every girl I dated to Jenny to the point where it completely took the fun out of it. When I wasn't able to distract myself with other girls, I decided it was best if I pulled back from Jenny a bit. We still talked a decent amount, but I avoided our usual FaceTime or Skype chats. I lied and told her that work was killing me, even though it hadn't been any busier than usual.

When I realized I needed to fly to California so I could visit a small surf shop at Venice Beach that had just connected with a large West Coast retailer, the first person I wanted to tell was Jenny. There was nothing that would have made me happier than spending a few extra days in the area just so I could have time with her and I knew that was exactly why I couldn't tell her. I felt guilty, but it's not like I was going to avoid her forever. I just needed this crush to die down and then things could go back to normal.

My thoughts were interrupted by Todd scooting into the booth across from me. "It took you long enough," I said with a little more attitude than I originally intended.

He shrugged his shoulders. "What did you expect Ror? I had no good excuse for why I was leaving for school two hours early today, so when my boyfriend held me up I couldn't exactly run out. It's not *my* fault we had to keep this little rendezvous a secret. I still don't understand why I'm the only one who is allowed to know that you are in California. Also, by the way, Jenny told me that you two haven't talked too much lately since you have been *oh so busy* with work. I find that funny since you have found plenty of time to talk to me."

Todd stared at me waiting for an explanation and when I didn't say anything, he continued. "What's going on with you Rory? I know you're avoiding Jenny. What happened?"

I shrugged my shoulders. "I don't want to talk about it." When Todd glared at me from across the table, I added, "As my best friend, isn't it your job to accept my decisions without questioning them?"

"Yes, but it's also my job to tell you when you're being an idiot and you, my dear, are being a big idiot."

I groaned and laid my head down on the table. After a

few seconds, I reluctantly lifted it back up and looked at Todd. "I like her Todd. Like I legitimately have a crush on her."

I held my breath as I waited for his response. To my surprise, he burst into a fit of laughter. I glared at him, but that wasn't enough to make him stop. Soon there were tears running down his cheeks because he was laughing so hard. After a few minutes, he finally stopped.

He put his hand on top of mine and smiled over at me. "I'm sorry to laugh at you but come on Rory. You're acting like this is some big revelation. I knew you loved this girl from the first time you told me about her."

I put up my hand to stop him. "Whoa there. No one said anything about love."

"Ok ok. Whatever. Let me rephrase that. I knew you had a *crush* on Jenny since the first time that cute face of yours lit up talking about her. So, what's the problem?"

"It's just...I have all of these feelings and.." Before I could continue, I was interrupted by Todd laughing again.

"I'm sorry Rory," he said in between giggles. "You just sound like the Grinch right now. What are you afraid of? That your heart is going to grow three sizes?"

I couldn't hold back a laugh, but I tried my best to hide it from Todd. "I'm not afraid of anything. I just don't want to ruin our friendship. Jenny has become one of my best friends."

"So pulling away from her and lying about where you are is your way of making sure your friendship isn't ruin? Makes perfect sense."

I rolled my eyes at his blatant sarcasm. "I'm giving my feelings the chance to die down so I don't end up doing something stupid. I'm not ruining our friendship for some stupid fling."

Todd studied me seriously for a few seconds. "Have you ever thought that maybe it wouldn't be a stupid fling? That maybe you could actually see yourself in a relationship?"

The truth was, I had thought about this. Lately, I started wondering more and more if I really did want to spend my whole life just casually dating. The idea didn't seem as logical anymore. Although, I would never admit that to Todd.

I shook my head at his question. "No, I can't see myself in a relationship," I lied. "But even if I could, Jenny is only into casual hookups and I respect that."

Luckily, Todd dropped the subject and updated me on what was new in his life instead. When we said our goodbyes he told me again what a big idiot he thought I was, but also promised to keep my trip a secret.

As soon as my plane landed back in Philadelphia, I noticed that my mom had called and texted me a few times. Once I was in my car, I called her back.

"Let me guess," I said as soon as she picked up. "You're calling to convince me to come home for thanksgiving. What is it? You don't feel like driving the two hours to my place?"

I was joking, but the silence on the other end of the phone made me believe that I might be right. "I'm sorry honey," my mom said quietly. "I just think we need to stay around here for the holidays this year."

"Why mom? What's going on?" Even as I asked the question, I was pretty sure I knew the answer, although I was hoping I was wrong.

"I didn't want to tell you this over the phone, but it's your grandpa," she confessed. "You know how he has been sick a lot lately? They just discovered that he has lung cancer and it's spreading. His body is just too old to fight it."

I held my head, knowing my worst nightmare had just come true. "How much time does he have Mom?"

She sighed. "He might have a few months, but he also might have a few weeks."

As soon as I hung up, I quickly stopped by my

apartment and threw a bunch of clothing into a suitcase, then headed back to my hometown. I called Todd on the way to update him on what was going on. By the time I pulled up to my mom's house, I had a text from Jenny telling me that she had heard the news and was here for me if I needed to talk. I should have known Todd wouldn't keep his big mouth shut, only this time I found myself thankful that he didn't.

The next two months flew by with me spending as much time with my grandpa as possible. Just a few days into January, I woke up in my old room to a weird feeling in the pit of my stomach. I knew something was wrong and slowly made my way down the stairs, not ready to find out what it was. My grandpa's health was rapidly deteriorating lately and it was obvious he only had a few days left.

When I walked into the kitchen, I found my mom holding the house phone in her hand with tears streaming down her face.

"Mom…" I said hesitantly. "Did grandpa pass away?"

She shook her head, but still didn't look up at me. "It's your..grandma… she… she.. had a.. a..heart attack."

I ran to the counter and picked up my keys, not worried about the fact that I was still wearing my pajamas. "Is she at the hospital? We need to get over there and see her.

Do you think she needs anything?"

My mom's tears turned into a sob and she shook her head. "No! No! No!" I practically shouted, catching on to what had happened. "But she was fine. She wasn't the one who was sick. She was fine. She has to be fine."

I almost fell over, but my mom stood up and held me in her arms. We embraced and cried together for a few minutes, until my mom backed up and wiped the tears from my eyes.

"We're meeting the rest of the family at the hospital," she informed me. "As soon as you're ready, we'll head over there."

I nodded and made my way up to my room, but before I started getting ready, I pulled out my phone to make a call. I knew that there was only one person I wanted to talk to right now.

After just two rings, Jenny picked up the phone. As if she could somehow read my mind and knew why I was calling, she spoke slowly and softly. "Hey Ror. Is everything ok?"

Before I could string any words together, I was crying again. Jenny, of course, assumed my grandpa had died and it took a few minutes for me to articulate that it was actually my grandma.

"Oh Ror, I'm so sorry," she apologized.

She reminded me that she would be there for me whenever I needed to talk and told me to call her as soon as I had some free time. Todd was right. I was an idiot for avoiding Jenny. I wish it hadn't taken a tragedy for me to realize that.

The next few hours dragged by. There was a lot of talk about how to handle my grandma's funeral and when it should take place. Even though no one was saying it, I knew they were dragging their feet because they had a feeling the funeral for one might turn into a funeral for two.

When I finally had a chance to look at my phone I had a text from Jenny. I was surprised by what she had said.

I spoke to Todd and my boss. We are going to fly in for the funeral. We want to be there for you. Just let us know when it is and we'll figure it out. I'm here for you Rory. Don't forget that.

Just two days later, it was confirmed that it would be a double funeral when my grandpa died in his sleep.

We planned the funeral for the following weekend and Todd and Jenny were able to get tickets to fly in the day before. There was so much that needed to happen leading up to the funeral that I felt like I had gone numb.

I was starting to wonder what was wrong with me, but as soon as I saw Jenny and Todd, the water works started all over again. Jenny took me in her arms and I melted into her. It felt good to be close to her, surrounded by the scent of her shampoo and body wash. It felt like home and for once, I didn't worry about what that meant. I needed her and, in that moment, everything felt right. When she finally pulled away from me, I immediately missed her even though she was still standing right in front of me. As I stared into her concerned eyes, I decided I would never let my feelings get in the way of what we had, whatever it was. As long as she wanted me around, I would be there, even if it meant ignoring the desire burning inside of me.

My thoughts were interrupted by the sound of Todd clearing his throat beside us. I had been so wrapped up in Jenny that I had honestly forgotten he was there. I gave him a quick hug and when I stepped back, my mom walked over to greet them. She gave Todd a big hug and a kiss on the forehead and told him how good it was to see him again. Then she walked over to Jenny and pulled her into a big hug as well.

"I'm looking forward to getting to know you better the next few days," I heard her whisper. "I didn't get to spend much time with you last time you were here."

Jenny stepped back and squeezed both of my mom's hands. "I'm looking forward to getting to know you too Mrs. Montgomery. I just wish it was under better circumstances."

We spent the day reminiscing about old memories of my grandma and grandpa with my family and feasting on the food that our neighbors had brought over. Around dinner time, the rest of my family left so I had time with just my mom, Todd, and Jenny.

Todd told my mom everything about Ryan and how in love he was. Then she asked Jenny questions about her family and job. As Jenny talked about some of the projects she was now doing at work, I realized just how much I had missed out on the past few months.

A few hours later, my mom yawned and announced that she needed to go to bed so she could be rested for the next day.

Todd looked at his watch. "I better go too. I need to catch my parents before they go to bed. I haven't seen them in months." He then turned to Jenny. "Do you want me to give you a ride to your cousin's house?"

Jenny nodded reluctantly as she looked over at me. I knew I wasn't doing a good job of masking my disappointment over them leaving, but I wasn't ready to be alone.

"Are you going to be ok?" Jenny asked, concern spread across her face.

"I think so," I lied, but my tone said otherwise.

"I could…" Jenny hesitated before continuing. "You know...stay here this weekend if you wanted me to. My aunt and uncle know I came here for you. I only said I would stay with them because I didn't want to intrude."

I was quiet for a few seconds as I contemplated Jenny's offer. All I wanted was to have Jenny close to me as much as possible, but was that really such a good idea?

Jenny must have taken my hesitation as a no because she stood up and started gathering her belongings. "You know what? I should probably just go. You and your mom don't need another person around here to add stress to your situation. I'll just see you tomorrow."

She started to turn around, but I reached out and grabbed her arm. "No. Don't go. Please stay with me."

I felt childish acting like this, but I couldn't help it. Jenny smiled at me and I stared into those shimmering brown eyes, feeling myself get lost for a minute.

"Sorry to interrupt this moment, but your bag is out in the rental car Jenny." I jumped at the sound of Todd's voice, but forced myself back to reality.

We followed Todd out to the car and I grabbed Jenny's bag for her. Before Todd got in, he winked at us. "You ladies have a good night. Don't do anything I wouldn't do."

I subtly lifted my middle finger at him so Jenny wouldn't see. He laughed and jumped into the car.

When we got back into the house, my eyes started to feel heavy and I suddenly realized how exhausted I was. I couldn't suppress a yawn from leaving my mouth.

"Should we get you to bed, pretty girl?" Jenny asked, putting her arm around my shoulder.

I tried to protest as she walked me in the direction of the stairs, feeling guilty that I had convinced her to stay when I couldn't even keep my eyes open. "No, it's fine. You stayed here so we could have more time together. We can hang out more."

Jenny shook her head. "I stayed so you would have me close by in case you needed anything."

I nodded my head and pointed to the room across from mine. "That's the guest room. You can stay there."

Jenny started heading toward the door and turned before entering. "I'm going to put my pajamas on and then I'll come over to say goodnight…. if that's ok. I just want to make sure you're ok before I go to sleep."

I tried my best to keep myself from visibly swooning over Jenny, but it was hard when she was being so sweet. "Of course that's ok. Thank you."

A few minutes after changing into a pair of shorts and a T-shirt, there was a knock on my door. When I opened up, Jenny was standing there wearing a pair of flannel pajama pants and a white t-shirt. Her hair was up in a ponytail and she was wearing glasses.

"Well, aren't these cute?" I teased while reaching out to touch her glasses.

She batted my hand away. "Shut up. I got up so early today. My contacts were killing me."

I shot her a half smile. "I kind of wish your contacts would kill you more often. I like this look on you. It's like nerd chic."

The slightest hint of blush spread across Jenny's cheeks. For a split second she looked shy and it was absolutely adorable. But all too quickly, a mischievous grin replaced her shy smile.

Before I could react, her hands were on my stomach tickling me. "Nerd chic, huh?"

I tried to squirm away, but her grip was too strong. I laughed so hard that tears started streaming down my face. I realized that this was the first time I had laughed in days and it felt good. I put my hands on Jenny's shoulders to try to push myself back, but her grip was too strong. She moved her hands down to my hips and held on tight. I stopped fighting her and looked into her eyes, very aware of her touch on the skin that was peeking out from under my t-shirt.

Jenny bit her bottom lip as she looked back into my eyes. She reached out a hand and moved a piece of hair behind my ear. She then leaned in close and took a deep breath. I could feel warm air in my ear and it sent chills through my body.

"We should get you to bed," Jenny whispered gently.

The thought of Jenny *putting me to bed* caused my chills to be replaced by a burning desire. I found myself wishing she hadn't meant it in the innocent way as I hopped into bed and crawled under the covers. I rolled onto my side so I was face to face with Jenny who was now kneeling beside my bed. She ran her hands through my hair as my eyes began to close. Soon I couldn't fight it anymore and started to drift off to sleep. When I entered the space between wake and sleep, Jenny moved her hand from my hair onto my cheek. I felt her move in closer and place a kiss on my forehead.

"Goodnight Ror," she whispered softly. "I hope you realize how much I care about you."

All I wanted to do was open my eyes and ask her just how much she did care about me. I was desperate to know if she cared about me in the same way I cared about her. But I couldn't fight the exhaustion and I fell asleep wondering if the feelings I thought I felt radiating in Jenny's words were all just a dream.

Chapter 12

I woke up the next day to the sound of someone knocking lightly on my bedroom door.

"Come in," I said groggily and looked up to see Jenny standing at the door, looking much more awake than I felt.

She laughed as I tried to fix my hair and wipe the drool off of my face. "Sorry to wake you sleeping beauty. The viewing starts in two hours, so your mom thought you would want to start getting ready."

I yawned again. "I'm surprised you're up. It's only 6:00 in California. Can I make you a coffee or something?"

Jenny held up the mug that I hadn't noticed in her hands. "I actually woke up about an hour ago." I was about to open my mouth to apologize, but Jenny waved a hand at me. "Don't worry about it. I was spending time with your mom. It was nice."

The thought of Jenny and my mom bonding made me unreasonably happy. It felt like she was my girlfriend who was important enough to meet my parents and that she was killing it with her future in laws. Except that wasn't the case at all. Jenny was just my friend. There was no future, aside from friendship. I was finding that I needed to remind myself of that more and more lately.

My thoughts were interrupted by a hand on my arm. I looked up to realize that Jenny was now leaning by my bed again, just like the night before.

"Are you ok?" She asked. "I was trying to talk to you and you completely zoned out."

"Sorry. I'm still half asleep," I lied.

She began to run her hand through my hair again and gave me a look I couldn't quite identify. She sighed softly as she closed her eyes. "You're irresistibly cute in the morning," she admitted.

I looked into her eyes as she opened them back up, watching them shimmer as she stared down at me. I looked at her lips and thought about how easy it would be to shorten the gap between us and finally feel her lips against mine. Jenny's eyes followed mine as if she was thinking the same thing.

"Girls," my mom's voice interrupted from downstairs. "I made some breakfast. You should eat something before we have to leave."

Jenny quickly jumped up and reached her hand down toward me. Once I was standing beside her, she immediately dropped my hand. "I'm really sorry. I shouldn't be flirting with you on the day of your grandparents' funeral."

"I mean do you know how not to flirt?" I tried to joke.

"I didn't think it was in your DNA to turn it off."

The serious look didn't leave Jenny's face. "I mean it Rory. You're my best friend. I wouldn't want you to think that you're just some girl that I like to sweet talk."

Hearing Jenny call me her best friend made me feel equal parts ecstatic and disappointed. It warmed me up inside knowing I was so important to her, but, no matter how hard I tried, I couldn't stop myself from wanting to be important to her in a different way.

"Are you kidding me?" I asked with a slight laugh. "You flew across the country to come to my grandparents' funeral. I don't think you would do that just so you could come sweet talk me. What would you be sweet talking me for anyway?"

Jenny cleared her throat and looked toward the floor. "Oh um.. yeah.. I wouldn't be. There would be no reason for that. We should get downstairs. Breakfast is going to get cold."

I put my hand on her arm before she could walk away. "I like this shy side of you. It's very endearing."

Jenny finally smiled again and placed her pointer finger on my chin dimple. "Who is the flirt now?"

I shrugged. "What can I say? It helps keep my mind off of things."

"I'll keep that in mind," Jenny said with a smirk and a wink, before making her way down the stairs to the kitchen. And just like that, she was back.

About twenty minutes before 11, we got into my mom's car and headed to the funeral home. The next two hours were going to be spent doing a viewing where people could come and pay their respect, then the funeral would immediately follow.

The viewing seemed to drag by as countless people made their way down the line of my family and all said the same sort of thing about how sorry they were and how hard it must have been to lose both of them in such a short time. It was nice to see how many people cared about my family, but it was also exhausting. The only thing that helped get me through was when I would look over to the seat that Jenny was sitting in and she would flash me an encouraging smile. The butterflies that would gather in my stomach every time were enough to keep my mind occupied for at least a few seconds.

Todd arrived with his parents a few minutes before the funeral was starting. I gave them all hugs and kisses and told them how much I appreciated having them all there. It was true. Todd's family had become like a second family to me through the years and his dad acted like much more of a father to me than my own, who had sent me his condolences through a text message. Jenny walked over and Todd introduced her. Jenny apologized for being partly at fault for their son moving across the country and we all laughed.

When it was time for the service to start, Jenny, Todd, and Todd's parents started heading toward seats a few rows back so my family could have the front. I found myself missing both of them during the service and wishing I had them as the words of the pastor brought tears to my eyes.

At the end of the service, they announced that the family and close friends would head to the cemetery for the burial, but we would meet the rest of the guests at my aunt and uncle's house for a cookout.

Todd's parents volunteered to get things together at their house so my aunt and uncle didn't have to worry about guests that would arrive before them. Todd followed us out to my mom's car and said that he wanted to be there for the burial.

The pastor said a few more words and my tears returned as the two caskets were lowered into the ground. My mom took my hand and we leaned on each other. Then I felt someone else take my other hand. The size of the hand and the fact that the contact didn't send a chill down my spine told me that it was Todd standing next to me. I squeezed his hand and forced a smile through my tears. I looked around at my family members and noticed that each of my aunts had their husband to lean on. I felt bad that my mom only had me. As I was watching my mom's empty side, I saw Jenny step up beside her and grab her hand. A look of deep appreciation appeared on my mom's face and I smiled over at Jenny to show her that I appreciated it as well.

After the funeral, we spent a few more hours entertaining guests at my aunt and uncle's house. The atmosphere was much more relaxed than the funeral, but it was still hard to deal with the constant looks of pity, even if they did come from a good place. After dinner time, we were finally able to head home. I said goodbye to Todd and his parents, who had been nice enough to stick around for the whole day, then headed home with my mom and Jenny. The car ride was quiet as we all silently reflected on the day.

When we got home, my mom told us she was exhausted from the past week and was going to call it an early night. Before heading upstairs, she turned around and looked to Jenny. "You're a really great person Jenny. I'm happy my daughter has you."

Jenny looked between my mom and I and smiled. "That means a lot to me Mrs. Montgomery. But I'm the lucky one. Rory is the greatest friend a girl could ask for."

I found myself cringing as she used the word friend again, but what did I expect? That's what we were.

Once my mom was upstairs, I pulled Jenny into my arms. I couldn't stop myself. It's all I wanted to do all day. "Thank you so much for everything," I whispered in her ear. "You've been so great to me and what you did for my mom at the burial was amazing."

Jenny squeezed me tight. "You're welcome. It was nothing though. I just felt like your mom could use a little extra support."

I pulled back so I could look into Jenny's eyes. "She did need the extra support, which is why you're so amazing. You were able to sense that and you went out of your way to make her comfortable."

Jenny shrugged her shoulders. "You mean a lot to me, so anything or anyone who is important to you, is important to me."

She then took my chin in her hand and squeezed it. "Plus your thankful smile is just so darn cute."

I raised an eyebrow at her. "What happened to the girl who apologized to me for flirting this morning?"

Jenny smiled slyly. "What can I say? I just can't control myself around you. Also, you said it took your mind off of things and I feel like you need that."

"More than you know," I said, moving across the room to sit on the couch.

Jenny sat down beside me and we sat silently for a few minutes before I spoke up. "My grandma died of a heart attack. She was always in such good health, then she found out my grandpa was sick and she had a heart attack. She literally died of a broken heart. I can't decide if that's beautiful or tragic."

Jenny grabbed my hand and I tried to ignore the feelings racing through me. "In a lot of situations, I'd say that's tragic. I hate that love and loss can affect someone that much. But in your grandparents' case, it's actually pretty beautiful. I mean from what I've heard, they both lived long, happy lives. Now they get to be together in the afterlife as well. Not that it makes things any easier for you."

"It does actually," I confessed. "I'm happy to know that they are together. As much as it sucks losing both of my grandparents at once, I don't think I could have dealt with watching one of them attend the other's funeral. It would have been completely heartbreaking."

"Can I ask you a question?" Jenny inquired, but continued before I could respond. "So to put it bluntly, it sounds like your parents had a super sucky relationship. And, understandably so, that turned you away from relationships.

But it looks like the rest of your family has solid relationships and I mean your grandparents clearly had a fairytale romance. So why does your parents' relationship trump what you've seen in all of these other relationships? I'm not judging. I'm just truly curious."

I tried to think of a good reason, but quickly realized that I didn't have one. "To be honest, I'm not sure," I admitted. "Maybe because they are the two people who have the biggest impact on my life. And I mean, it's not like I don't believe in love. I've seen a lot of really beautiful relationships so I know how great it can be. Unfortunately, I also know how terrible it can be. The risk never seemed worthwhile. At least, that's how I used to feel."

I cringed when I realized I had said the last part out loud and prayed that Jenny didn't notice.

She tilted her head in confusion. Of course she heard it. "What are you trying to say Rory?"

I tried to force a laugh. This certainly wasn't the conversation I wanted to have right now or any time for that matter. "I'm not sure what I'm trying to say. I think all of the emotions are messing with my brain. I don't know what I'm thinking." When she didn't look pleased with my answer I added, "I know one thing though. I'm not ready for you to leave tomorrow."

Jenny sighed. "I know. I wish I could stay longer. I just have a lot going on at work right now."

I nodded. "I completely understand that. I'm just thankful that you were able to come at all. It's just hard not knowing when I'll be seeing you next."

Jenny's eyes lit up a bit. "That actually reminds me. My sister got engaged a few months ago. Sorry I didn't say anything. You were just so busy with work that I didn't have the chance. But anyway, the wedding is in June and my sister said I could bring a guest. Ok, that's a lie. She actually requested that I bring you. Apparently she thought you were really funny at John and Valerie's wedding. I personally think she's crazy, but hey, what can I do? Bride's request!"

"I would love to Jenny," I answered quickly.

"Are you sure?" She questioned. "If work is too busy, you don't have to. You don't seem overly excited about it."

"Sorry, I am. I really am. I can't wait. That's the problem. I was just thinking how much this situation sucks. You know, seeing each other for just a few days then going months before we see each other again for a few more days," I admitted.

"It does suck. But what can we do? We live on opposite sides of the country."

We both sat in silence like we were contemplating the

question and then a strange look came onto Jenny's face. "So I have a kind of crazy idea. Since you work from home anyway, what would you think about coming to California for a few weeks before the wedding? You could stay with your dad to get some extra time with him and then you and I would get to see each other a lot too. And it's not like you're choosing him over your mom since you're not actually moving to California."

I smiled at Jenny as my stomach did somersaults. "It sounds like you thought of everything. Except one little detail unfortunately. My dad and Monica are apparently going backpacking through Europe for three months starting in May. I thought that was something only people our age did, but whatever. Either way, he won't be there. I'm sure he would let me stay at his house though."

Jenny shook her head. "I don't want to make you stay in his big house by yourself. You're already going to be living in a place that's far from most of your friends and family." She hesitated before adding, "You know, I did get a pull out couch for my apartment. My place obviously isn't the biggest, but Ryan and I made it work living there together. You could.. stay with me… if you wanted to."

Everything inside of me was telling me that this was a terrible idea so I was shocked when my mouth started moving and I found myself saying, "What the heck? Let's do it! That sounds like fun."

I'm not sure what part of pining over Jenny while we lived in such close quarters sounded like fun, but it seemed like the only option. Now that the thought of having more time with her was in my mind, I couldn't imagine not going through with it.

The next day when Todd picked up Jenny so they could head to the airport, I did my best not to mention my trip. Todd was obviously going to find out, but I needed to figure out the right way to tell him.

Later that night, almost immediately after Jenny texted to tell me that they made it back safely, a call came through from Todd.

He cut right to the chase without even saying hello. "Jenny and I had a very interesting conversation on the plane. She told me all about this trip you guys planned for May."

"Yeah, about that…" I started to say but was interrupted by Todd snickering loudly.

"Let me break it down for you," Todd quipped. "Just a few months ago, you were doing everything in your power to avoid this girl. Now you are flying across the country to shack up with her. You're losing your mind."

I opened my mouth to argue with him, but realized I

had nothing to fight back with. He was right. I had completely lost my mind and was in way over my head, but it was too late to turn back now.

Chapter 13

I felt nervous excitement building up inside me as I waited outside of the LA airport for Jenny to pick me up.

"Hey pretty lady. Looking for a ride?" Jenny shouted out the window as she drove up.

I made a face like I was thinking about it. "I don't know. I'm kind of on the lookout for a really gorgeous California girl who enjoys a good party, but is also down to stay at home and watch High School Musical with me."

"It looks like it's your lucky day," Jenny said as she got out of the car and wrapped me in her arms. I squeezed her tighter against me and then pulled back so I could look into her stunning eyes.

When I found myself getting lost in those eyes, I forced myself to look away. If I was going to survive this living situation, I was going to have to learn how to keep my feelings under control.

Jenny looked over toward my three bags and rolled her eyes. "Well gee.. do you think you brought enough?" She poked me in my stomach as she teased me.

"You know, instead of making fun of me, you could be a good hostess and offer to help me with said bags."

As Jenny bent down to pick up my bag, her v neck

slipped down to reveal the very top of her black lace bra. Every part of my body felt like it was on fire, but I willed myself to look away. Unfortunately, I was too late.

"Enjoying the view?" Jenny asked while tilting her head up at me.

"Oh. I wasn't. I mean…"

My stuttering was interrupted by Jenny's laughter. "Might as well get used to it if we're going to be living together for the next month."

I smiled slyly at her, trying to make up for my stuttering. "I mean, it is a great view," I said flirtatiously.

Jenny put my bag into the car then moved her eyes up and down my body, causing another bolt of electricity to pulse through me. "The view from over here isn't so bad either."

We put the other two bags into the car, then headed toward Jenny's apartment. When we arrived, I dropped my bags at the door and took in my surroundings. It felt different from the last time I was there knowing this would be my house for the next three weeks until we left to spend a week back in Jenny's hometown for her sister's wedding.

Jenny wrapped her arms around me from behind and rested her chin on my shoulder. "So, what do you think? Think you'll be able to turn this small space into your office for the next few weeks?"

"It's perfect Jenny," I answered sincerely. "It already feels like home."

Jenny smiled and closed her eyes, chin still rested on my shoulder. "It does, doesn't it?"

She drew in a deep breath through her nose and I couldn't decide if she was taking in her surroundings or taking in me. I know which one of those I was hoping for.

Since it was Sunday, we spent the rest of the night relaxing on the couch. Before long, neither of us could keep our eyes open. Jenny helped me with the pull out couch and tucked me in just as she had a few months prior.

"I'm sorry I have to work so much while you're here," she apologized while running her hand through my hair. "I couldn't get anymore days off since I'm taking the week for my sister's wedding."

"Don't even worry about it." *If every night ends like this, I'm completely ok with it.* "I'm just happy with any time we have together."

The next day when Jenny got home from work, she was surprised to find that I had gone grocery shopping and cooked dinner for us.

One of the benefits of having a stay at home job was that I could do things like this and we quickly fell into a pattern. Everyday, Jenny would leave for work and I would get up to do my work for the day. Once I was done, I would either make dinner or order something for us. We normally spent the rest of the night watching tv, playing board games, or just talking. The nights spent talking were my favorites. Jenny told me all about her family and I found myself getting more and more excited to officially meet them. Every night, Jenny continued to tuck me into bed and kiss me on the forehead to say goodnight. It was completely platonic, but still extremely sweet and made my heart play tricks on me.

Our weekends were spent with Todd and Ryan either sightseeing or going to the beach. For whatever reason, none of us were feeling LA nightlife at the time so we spent most evenings in.

The night before we were leaving for Jenny's hometown, right after she had headed into her own room, I said a silent prayer thanking God that I had her in my life. All of my worries from the past year were starting to disperse. If we could make it through three weeks of living together with no one else around and not have any almost moments, I guess we could just be friends. Yep. We had made it through the toughest challenge and I hadn't let my feelings ruin this friendship. Nothing could possibly go wrong now.

Chapter 14

My nerves got the best of me as we pulled up to Jenny's childhood home and I could feel myself starting to sweat. Jenny must have noticed because she looked at me with a raised eyebrow.

"What's up with you?" She asked. "You look like you're about to throw up."

"I just really want your family to like me," I admitted. "You're so important to me and they are important to you so I want to make a good impression."

Jenny put her hand on top of mine and gave me a reassuring smile. "They already like you. They've heard so much about you, I'm sure they feel like they already know you." I felt excited over the prospect of Jenny telling her family about me but that excitement died when she added, "I mean they visited LA a few months ago and we spent time with Todd and Ryan so your name came up a lot."

As soon as we were inside, a little boy with blonde curly hair came running toward us.

"Auntie Jen," he screamed excitedly as he jumped into Jenny's arms.

Jenny showered him with kisses and then started to tickle him. "Man Patrick. You're so big. How old are you now? 25? Did you graduate from college yet?"

He laughed as he tried to wiggle his way out of her arms. "No silly. I'm four."

Just as she put him back down, a little girl with curly brown hair and shimmering brown eyes just like Jenny's ran up to her.

"Me next," she begged with outstretched arms.

Jenny picked her up and repeated the same process with her as tears ran down the little girl's face in laughter. I got lost in the moment and stared at Jenny, picturing her doing that with our.. I mean… her.. children.

Jenny looked over at me and caught me staring. "Take a picture. It lasts longer."

"Hardy har. Good one," I joked, trying to hide my embarrassment of being caught once again. "I was just thinking about how much she looks like you."

"Yep, she definitely has those Hanson family genes," I heard another voice say. I turned to see a short petite blonde enter the hallway.

She immediately walked over to Jenny and wrapped her in a big hug. "I didn't think I would see you guys tonight," Jenny said as they pulled apart.

A guy who looked like the male form of Jenny then walked into the room and put his arm around her. "Are you kidding me? I couldn't miss the opportunity to welcome home my kid sister. We never see you anymore now that you're living that movie star life in Hollywood."

He then turned to me and reached out his hand. "You must be Rory. I'm Jenny's brother, Jake. It's so nice to finally meet you."

I shook his hand and he elbowed Jenny in the ribs. "This one here wouldn't stop talking about you when we came to visit her a few months ago. It was all 'Rory this' and 'Rory that.' You're even prettier than she described though, which is hard to believe with the way she talked about you."

Jenny glared at her brother as her face turned more red than I had ever seen it before. She gained composure and pointed to the petite blonde. "Rory, this is my sister in law Ashley."

She bent down to get on the same level as her niece and nephew and hugged them close. "And these two cuties are Patrick and Kelsey. Can you guys give Rory a hug?"

They did as instructed and when I stood back up from hugging them, another girl close to our age who also looked a lot like Jenny, came running into the room. She had her arms spread open and I was sure she was rushing to give Jenny a hug, but was surprised when I found myself tangled in her tight embrace.

"Rory! It's so nice to meet you," she said without letting go. "I'm Jasmine. I'm so happy you could come for my wedding."

She pulled back, keeping her hands locked on my arms, then looked at Jenny with a mischievous grin. "You were right Jenny. This girl is stunning."

She turned back to me and winked while Jenny's face turned red once again.

"Oh, I didn't," Jenny began to say, but was interrupted by the sound of a motherly voice.

"Would you kids please stop making fun of your sister? She'll never come home if this is how she gets greeted."

She gave Jenny a kiss on the forehead, then turned to me and opened her arms. "Rory! So great to meet you. Incase you haven't noticed, we're a hugging family."

While I was in the middle of hugging her, I felt a strong hand land on my back. I turned around to see a man who looked like the older, more gray version of Jenny's brother. He smiled and flashed me a friendly wink. "It's great to have you here Rory. We're all looking forward to getting to know you better."

Jenny rolled her eyes at her family and grabbed my arm, directing me toward the staircase. "Calm down people.

Let's give our guest the chance to breathe, ok?"

I tried my best to offer them an appreciative grin as Jenny pulled me up the stairs. Once we were in her room, she let go of my arm.

"I'm really sorry about them," she apologized. "They can be a bit much at times, but I promise that they really do mean well."

I snickered at her apology. "Jenny there is nothing to be sorry about. Your family is great. I can already tell that I'm going to get along with them."

The truth was that I could already tell that her family was the type of family I had always dreamed of being a part of. All of those times I would listen to my parents fighting, I would picture a happy family, including lots of teasing siblings and loving parents. My mom did everything she could for me, but this was of course something that she could never give me. I wasn't going to share any of this with Jenny though. For some reason, admitting that I wanted a family like hers seemed too intimate.

"I'm glad you feel that way, because the truth is, we only have a few more minutes up here before someone comes looking for us. Yes, they are that crazy," she explained with a giggle.

I nodded in understanding, then studied Jenny's room.

I noted that she had very few pictures. There was a double frame that had two pictures of her and Allison in graduation caps and gowns, which I had to assume were from high school and college. There was one picture of her whole family at what looked like her brother's wedding and then another of just her and her siblings at the beach when they were younger. The walls were covered in inspirational quotes. It kind of looked like tumblr had exploded on her wall, with pictures of landscapes such as mountains containing the words like "The best view comes after the hardest climb." The mirror of her vanity was adorned with notecards that she had written herself reminders on. I read one that said "Reminder: You deserve to be happy" and was about to read the next when I was interrupted by a knock at the door.

Jenny opened it up and her parents were standing there with my bags. Her dad lifted up the two that were in his hands. "We figured we should drop these off for you," he proclaimed.

"I hope you don't mind sharing a room with Jenny this week," her mom added. "Jasmine isn't moving out until after the wedding and Jake has been gone so long that we actually turned his old room into an office." Her face turned red like she was embarrassed that they had redone the room of her grown son.

I told them not to worry about it, then Jenny and I followed them downstairs, knowing they would probably find any excuse to come back. After dinner, Jake's family said their goodbyes and Mrs. Hanson asked if we wanted to play a game of charades. Jenny and Jasmine quickly agreed, leading me to believe that this wasn't anything out of the ordinary with their family.

Mr. Hanson decided it should be kids vs adults and when our last turn rolled around, the game was tied. Jenny picked a card and a wicked grin entered her face. When the timer started, she held up two fingers to indicate that it was two words and then flashed the two fingers again to show that she would be giving clues for the second word. She pointed to a calendar and Jasmine and I started rattling off words until I shouted the word "day" and she gave me a thumbs up. Next, she held up one finger to confirm that we were moving on to the first word. She started doing a humping motion and made a face while sticking her tongue out. Although it was absolutely ridiculous and meant to be funny, I could still feel my face turning red at the thought of Jenny doing what she was demonstrating to something, or rather someone, other than the air.

"Hump," her sister squeaked out between giggles.

"Hump day!"

They high fived as her mom shook her head. "Jennifer Anneliese Hanson! That was completely inappropriate young lady."

Now it was Jenny's turn to get a red face, although I had a feeling it wasn't because of her mom scolding her because Mrs. Hanson immediately started to giggle despite herself when Jenny retorted, "Oh stop. You're just mad because you lost."

"Jennifer Anneliese Hanson, huh?" I remarked with a smirk once we were back in Jenny's room.

She pointed a stern finger at me. "Don't you ever repeat that again. You got it?"

"Aw why not? I think it's adorable." And it really was. But then again, anything about Jenny was adorable to me.

Before I knew it, Jenny's hands were on my sides tickling me. I began gasping for air as the laughter poured out of me. "Tell me you'll never repeat that again," Jenny demanded as she dug her fingers in.

"Fine," I said between breaths. "I'm... done.. I.. won't.. say it."

"That's what I thought," Jenny said with a smug grin.

I went to the bathroom to change and brush my teeth

and by the time I returned, Jenny was already tucked underneath the covers. I took a blanket out of my bag, laying it across the floor, then motioned to the pillow laying beside Jenny.

"Mind if I use that?" I asked.

Jenny looked from the pillow to the blanket and then back at me. "I can't make you sleep on the floor. You're my guest. You can… you know… share the bed with me."

I stared at the bed longingly, but shook my head. "Didn't we have this same talk a few years ago when you tried to get me in bed with you? I stand by what I said back then. It's not a good idea."

Jenny rolled her eyes at me. "Oh come on. So much has changed since then. We're older and more mature. Plus, we've been friends for so long now, I think we can handle it." She stared at me for a moment then added, "But if you're going to be stubborn, I'm still not going to make you sleep on the floor. I will be the one to sleep there. You're my guest."

I sighed. "I'm not going to make you do that," I remarked as I crawled onto the other side of the bed. "But don't go getting handsy on me," I joked, knowing my words didn't match what I was currently feeling.

"I wouldn't dream of it," Jenny mocked. "Ok. That's

a lie. I'm totally going dream about it, but I won't do it."

With a wink, she rolled over to face the opposite direction and I didn't hear another peep out of her the rest of the night.

The rest of the week flew by with Hanson family time and last minute wedding preparations. I was never around another family that was as close as Jenny's. Even Todd's close knit family didn't seem to share the same bond.

Somehow I was able to survive the nights spent laying just inches away from Jenny. It certainly helped that we both squeezed to the edge on our respective sides of her queen size bed, but that wasn't enough to completely kill the desire inside of me. Baby steps. This was another good test. Another one that I happened to be passing.

When the day of the wedding came, I helped Mr. and Mrs. Hanson put the finishing touches on their house, where Jasmine had decided to have her wedding. There was a large tent covering just a small fraction of their acres of backyard space. Under the tent, the dance floor, dj booth, and tables were set up. The ceremony space was just a few feet away from this.

When the time got close for the wedding to begin, I took a seat near the back of the rows of chairs. As I stared ahead, I felt someone scoot in beside me and elbow me in the ribs.

"Hey Cous. Fancy seeing you here," Valerie remarked, not seeming nearly as surprised as I would have expected her to.

"Val," I replied excitedly. "I didn't think about the fact that you would be here. This is so great."

"Yeah, it's shocking to think that I would be at my cousin in law's wedding," she remarked with an eye roll.

Before I had the chance to reply, the ceremony started. I smiled as each member of Jenny's family walked down the aisle, the smile growing exponentially when it was Jenny's turn. The knee length rose gold dress looked stunning on her. It was a flattering dress that looked nice on the whole bridal party, but the way it hugged her curves was better than anyone else. As I stared at her, I felt an elbow come into my side again.

"So, are you guys going to get married at the old homestead also?" Valerie whispered as she leaned in close.

I scowled at her. "It's not like that between us and you know it," I whispered back.

She patted my hand. "Whatever you say Rory," she teased.

Valerie was the only person I knew who could tease someone relentlessly and still look sweet doing it. It must have been the perfect Christian girl persona spilling out of her. For that reason, I couldn't even get mad when she squeezed my hand and giggled every time she caught my eyes lingering on Jenny, which happened to occur throughout most of the ceremony.

I spent the cocktail hour catching up with Valerie and John while Jenny and the rest of the bridal party got pictures taken.

When it was time for introductions, we found a table that the three of us could sit at together since Jenny was going to be sitting at the bridal party head table. Since I had a feeling Valerie wasn't going to back off of the teasing during dinner, I went to the bar and had two mixed drinks made, gulping one down before I even got to the table.

When Valerie caught me with one empty cup and one half empty cup, she lifted an eyebrow at me. "Be careful Jenny," she warned. "You know what they say about alcohol."

"You mean what the Bible says in 1st Timothy, that we shouldn't just drink water, but instead wine, for our ailments?"

I smirked cockily, feeling very proud of myself. I always loved when I could come at my cousin with bible verses. Sometimes I felt guilty, wondering if this was the only reason I actually read the Bible, since most of it seemed to be over my head.

"Good one. And as proud as I am that you are quoting the Bible to me right now, that's not what I meant. I meant that little saying about alcohol making you more honest. You know… causing you to admit your actual feelings. Feelings you have for a certain maid of honor who happens to look stunning in her dress."

I felt my face turning red, but instead of saying anything, I quickly finished the rest of my drink. I held it up toward her. "And on that note, I'm going to get another drink."

I went to the bar and ordered two more, not because I particularly wanted any truth to come out, but rather I just wanted to forget about that longing ache and my cousin's teasing wasn't helping.

By the time the introductions, toasts, and dances were through and Jenny finally had a chance to come to our table, I had a pretty decent buzz going.

I grabbed her hand and pulled her down to my level. "Has anyone told you yet that you look absolutely stunning in that dress?"

"Someone has actually," she said apologetically. When my face fell, she added, "But it was my mom so I'm not quite sure if that counts."

She looked me up and down in a way that had my heart racing, then shot me her signature half smile. "I must say though, you clean up quite well yourself," she flirted.

She caught up with Valerie and John, then apologetically said her goodbyes when the food arrived, promising to talk to us more after dinner.

Before she left, she placed a hand on my shoulder and winked. "Save a dance for me pretty girl?"

"I'll save every dance for you," I retorted before I could think my words through. I cringed as soon as the words left my mouth.

Luckily, Jenny just giggled and patted my shoulder. "You also might want to save some alcohol for the rests of the guests," she joked before walking away.

Valerie gave me a smug look and I pushed my unfinished drink out of the way.

"I think I'll switch to that water now," I quipped sarcastically.

Once the dance floor opened up, I immediately headed out there to dance off my buzz. I grabbed everyone and anyone who was willing to dance with me. Yep, no bad decisions would be made tonight.

Near the end of the night, someone grabbed me and

twirled me around. When I came face to face with the person, I realized it was Jasmine. After spending a few songs seeing who could do the most ridiculous dance moves, the DJ announced it was time for the last song. To my surprise, a slow song began playing. I never understood why people would want to end a fun reception with a slow song, but to each their own. I started to look around the room for Jenny, but Jasmine draped her arms around my shoulders instead.

"Don't you want to dance with your husband?" I asked while we swayed to the music.

"Eh. I have my whole life to dance with him. This gives us a chance to talk."

I gulped, wondering what Jasmine wanted to talk to me about.

After a few agonizing moments, Jasmine finally started to speak again. "I'm really glad you could be part of this. It's been awesome to finally get to know you. I've heard so much about you from my sister over the past few years."

"Thank you for having me," I said, relaxing a bit. "Spending time with your family this week was wonderful. It's easy to see why family is so important to Jenny. You guys are all so loving and accepting. She's lucky to have you."

"Funny. I was about to tell you how lucky she is to

have you. I've never seen my sister as happy as she is when you're around. After she graduated from high school, I always worried how much of her happiness was sincere, but I don't have to wonder that when you're around. She sparkles around you."

Before I could think of how to respond, I felt a hand on my shoulder. "Mind if I cut in?" Jenny asked.

"She's all yours," her sister said with a wink. Jenny gave her a kiss on the cheek, before grabbing me and pulling me in close to her.

"I didn't think I was going to get a dance with you. My own sister got a dance before me. I'm hurt," she joked.

"What can I say? You Hanson women can't get enough of me."

Jenny sighed. "It's true. I'm surprised my mom isn't over here asking you for a dance."

"Oh guess what?" Jenny added excitedly. "One of my dad's friends was telling me about a small diner in LA called Faye's. I figured next time you come to visit, we should try it. Have you ever heard of it?"

"Oh yeah. Todd and I had breakfast at that diner just a few…" I let myself trail off before I could finish my statement.

"Weird. I didn't realize you and Todd went out to

breakfast. Was that some morning that I was working?" There was nothing accusatory about her voice. Just actual curiosity. I knew I could lie and she would never know. But I didn't want to lie to Jenny.

"No, that's actually not when we went," I whispered while looking down at the floor. I looked back up at Jenny and added, "Do you think we could talk about this a little later? In private?"

Jenny looked confused, but not hurt or mad. "You're being super weird right now. But yeah, of course we can." She then leaned in closer to me and whispered, "By the way, no offense to my sister, but if I was ever going to have a wedding it would NOT end with a slow dance. What a buzzkill."

I tried my best to laugh, but inside my stomach was tying into knots. I had to find a way to explain to this perfect girl why I was avoiding her without spilling to her just how perfect I really thought she was.

Chapter 15

After all of the guests left and we had helped with cleaning up, Jenny and I headed up to her bedroom. We both changed into pajamas and I paced around the room as I waited for her to return from the bathroom.

"What is going on with you?" Jenny asked as she walked back into the room. "You've been weird ever since the last dance. Is this about the diner? Are you going to divulge the details of your super secret diner trip?"

She grinned from ear to ear as I walked over to her and placed my hands on her arms.

I cleared my throat a few times before formulating my confession. "The truth is, Todd and I actually went to that diner back in November."

Jenny's face scrunched up like she was thinking. "I don't get it. You haven't been in LA since your dad's wedding last summer." She thought for a few more seconds and then her face dropped. "Unless you came to LA and didn't tell me."

I stared at a quote on her wall about never giving up in order to avoid seeing the hurt in her eyes. "I'm sorry. It was a really short trip. I needed to come for work and was literally in town for less than 48 hours."

"Ok…" Jenny stretched out the word. "But we still could have figured out a time to see each other, even if it was really quick. Didn't you want to see me?"

I let out a frustrated sigh. She wasn't going to make this easy on me and truthfully, I deserved it. "Of course I wanted to see you Jenny. I just couldn't, ok?"

"That doesn't make sense Rory." I could hear anger starting to build in Jenny's voice. I had never experienced her being angry before. "You wanted to see me but you couldn't. Were you actually even super booked with work all those months you told me you didn't have any time to video chat?"

"Honestly, I wasn't any busier than usual. I just had some…stuff..going on. I'm really sorry Jenny. It was stupid and I realize that now. I realized how dumb I was being right after I left LA. I regret it. I really do. But you have to know that it had nothing to do with you. It was all me." I knew I was rambling now, but I couldn't stop myself.

Jenny was trying to keep her voice calm, but I noticed the shakiness behind it. "If it has nothing to do with me, then just tell me what was going on with you. You know you can tell me anything."

"I… I just… can't tell you this." My voice cracked as the words came out and I tried to keep myself from crying.

Jenny's voice was no longer calm. She was clearly

pissed. "What the hell Rory?! You literally make no sense. You're going on and on about how this was all about you and what you were going through. Yet, you still made time for Todd so clearly it has something to do with me. So just tell me. Tell me why you would try to avoid me for months. Tell me why you would fly all the way to LA and not say a damn word to me. Tell me why I was suddenly not good enough to be around."

By the end, she was shouting and I found myself bubbling over as well. I knew I was probably going to regret the words that were about to come out of my mouth, but I couldn't stop them.

"Do you really want to know why? I didn't tell you because every time I'm with you, all I can think about is how much I want to kiss you. Heck, it's so much more than that. I want to hold you and tell you how pretty you look. I want to take you on dates and hold your hand while we eat dinner. I thought if I pulled back a little these feelings would go away. I know that's not what you want and it's confusing, because it's normally not what I want either. But pulling away didn't work so now I don't know what to do because I don't want to ruin what we have. You're so important to me and I just...."

Before I could finish my sentence, Jenny's lips were on mine. It took me a few seconds to register what was happening, but once my brain caught up with my mouth, I put my hands on her hips and pulled her closer. I didn't know exactly what was happening, but I knew this was the best damn kiss of my entire life. I opened my mouth to hers and moaned as our tongues met for the first time. Every part of my body was on fire. Jenny pushed me up against the wall as I kept my hands on her hips so there wasn't even an inch of space between our bodies. She moved her hands into my hair and pulled at it lightly as she bit my bottom lip, before bringing her tongue back into my open mouth. I'm not sure how long this lasted, but at some point we broke apart to catch our breath. I kept my eyes closed for a few seconds, not wanting the moment to end and worried if I opened them I would find it was all just a dream. I finally opened my eyes when I felt Jenny's forehead against mine. To my surprise, Jenny's eyes were still closed and a small smile played on her swollen lips. When she opened her eyes, her smile widened as our eyes made contact. Just as quickly, the color started to drain from Jenny's face and her smile faded.

"Shit," she whispered as she backed away from me. "Shit shit shit. I'm sorry. I never meant for that to happen."

She ran a hand through her hair and then began to rub her forehead. "You were just saying all the right things. Everything you said put exactly how I've been feeling into words. Then I just lost all control."

I cupped her cheeks between my hands and forced her to look at me. "Hey. Calm down. It's going to be ok. Just breathe."

Jenny took a deep breath, then moved away from my touch. She looked down at the ground as she spoke. "I can't do this Rory. That can't happen again. Whatever this is between us - I can't do it. I can't have these feelings. I can't get hurt again."

With that last sentence, her shoulders started to shake and I realized she was crying. Instinctively, I reached out and took her into my arms. She put her head onto my shoulder and sobbed. I held her tight until I started to feel her pull away.

I took her hand in mine. "Talk to me. Tell me what's going on."

Jenny looked at me with red rimmed eyes. "I'm scared," she admitted. "I haven't let myself have feelings for someone since high school and at that time, I vowed I never would."

"This person you had feelings for..." I hesitated. "She's the reason you don't date."

Jenny nodded her head and looked back down at the ground.

"You don't have to talk about it if you don't want to," I informed her.

She looked at me and the slightest smile returned to her face. "No, I want to. It was a big part of my life and you should know what happened. You deserve to know why I'm such an ice queen when it comes to feelings."

Jenny took a few minutes to gather her thoughts before she started speaking again.

"When I was in 6th grade a girl named Tonya McGregor moved into my neighborhood. She instantly became my best friend and together we made more friends. I didn't really have any close friends before she came around. I was quiet and kind of a loner, while Tonya was confident and outspoken. By the end of middle school, all of my friends, including Tonya, started being interested in guys. I figured I just hadn't reached that point yet, like maybe I was a late bloomer. I asked my one friend what it felt like to have a crush on a guy and I realized that all the feelings she was describing were feelings I had for Tonya. I tried to blow it off for awhile, but by the middle of freshman year, I couldn't deny it to myself anymore. I knew I liked Tonya and kind of figured that must have meant that I was gay. I decided I was going to keep this newly discovered part to myself. The only friend that I felt close enough with to tell was Tonya and I was afraid she would figure out that I liked her if she knew I was gay. So the plan was to just keep it to myself during high school and then give myself a fresh start in college by coming out."

Jenny stopped her story to take a few more deep breaths. She looked toward the ceiling and tried to blink away tears before continuing.

"It was weird though. I started to notice that Tonya treated me differently from our other friends. She always had to be touching me in some way, whether it was a hand on my arm or her head on my shoulder. I thought maybe I was just imagining it, but then Tonya pre-gamed before going to our high school's first football game our sophomore year. She was completely hammered and I worried she would get in trouble, so I drove her home during halftime. When we got to her house, I helped her change into pajamas and tucked her into bed. Right before I was about to turn around to leave, she grabbed me and kissed me. I didn't really react because I was so shocked and I also didn't want to take advantage of her when I was sober. The next day, she didn't acknowledge what happened. It continued like that until she got drunk again and repeated the kiss. It became a pattern that every time she drank she would get me alone and kiss me. I noticed that with each kiss though, it took less and less alcohol for her to do it. Our first real sober kiss came that New Year's Eve. It was one of the many times she had sworn off drinking so she asked if I wanted to stay in with her. When midnight came, she kissed me and I swore I saw fireworks. We got into a heated make out session that lasted until the sun came up."

I took a big gulp of air. I was starting to figure out why Jenny and I never talked about our sexual encounters. She was telling me about a pg make out session she had in high school and I still felt jealous for some reason. I looked over to Jenny and nodded for her to keep going.

"After that, we found any excuse to be alone so we could kiss or even just snuggle. Every time, Tonya would say she was just practicing for her future boyfriends, but the way she would hold me in her arms and look at me made me believe differently."

Jenny paused again and this time the tears flowed freely. I had a feeling the next part of the story would be the big "but" where everything fell apart. I rubbed her back to show her that I was there for her.

"About two weeks before our junior year, my parents went away for the weekend and I asked Tonya to sleepover. It started out innocently enough with us just making out and feeling each other up over our clothes. But slowly we ended up taking off our clothes and..well.. that was the night I lost my virginity. I had known I was in love with Tonya for a few months, but decided I could finally tell her. Apparently, I was wrong. As soon as I said it she dashed out of my house and I didn't hear from her again. I texted and called her countless times over the next week and when that didn't work, I decided to send her a Facebook message so I could at least see when she read it. I poured my heart out in that message telling her how long I had liked her, and now loved her, and that I was willing to do anything to be with her. Looking back, I can see how pathetic that was, but at the time it felt like the right thing to do."

"Hey," I said reassuringly. "You were in love. You did what your heart felt was right. You can't blame yourself for that."

Jenny tried to smile at me, but I could tell it was forced. "She read my message almost immediately, but again, didn't respond. I figured I could just talk to her once school started again. But when I got to school on that first day, I found out that Tonya had printed out multiple copies of the message I wrote her and was passing it out to everyone in the school."

I scrunched up my nose in thought. "I don't get it though. Wouldn't that note have outed her too?"

Jenny laughed sarcastically. "That was the best part. She whited out all of the parts that could have been incriminating to her so it just looked like I was weirdly obsessed. She told people that the missing parts were where I talked about other girls I had big lesbian crushes on and she figured she would save them the embarrassment."

I shook my head in disbelief. "And people actually believed that?"

"Yep. Every single one of my friends did at least. Except for Allison. We had always run with the same group, but we weren't super close until this happened. She pulled me aside and told me that she didn't care that I was gay or that I was in love with Tonya. She was the only person willing to stick up for me to the rest of our friends, or the rest of the student body for that matter."

"But didn't you still have the copy of the Facebook message?" I asked. "You could have shown people the original with the parts that involved Tonya."

Jenny sighed. "I didn't only have the Facebook message. I also had some texts saved from Tonya where she told me how much she liked kissing me."

"So, did you show those to people?"

Jenny shook her head. "Only Allison. But not until after I knew that she had my back. She tried to convince me to show people the messages, but I refused."

"But why wouldn't you?" I asked, completely aghast.

Jenny shrugged her shoulders. "I didn't feel like I owed those people anything. They were so quick to believe Tonya and turn on me. I already knew they weren't true friends, so I decided they weren't worth my time."

"Good for you," I said with a smile.

Jenny laughed sarcastically again. "Yeah. If only I actually didn't let them get to me. I couldn't deal with the bullying and whispers and started to feel really depressed. The hardest part though was that my heart was completely broken. It was like Tonya had flipped a switch and become a completely different person. She could walk by me in the hall and look right past me. The only times she acknowledged me was to call me dyke or queer. That New Year's Eve, I told Allison I was staying in and I sat at home honestly considering whether or not I wanted to be alive anymore. All I could think about were the last two years that I had spent with Tonya and didn't see how I could get past it, especially since everyone in the school seemed set on making my life miserable. Allison ended up coming to my house that night. She told me that she was worried about me and didn't want to leave me alone. That's when I broke down and told her about the thoughts I was having. She convinced me to tell my family and they were able to get me help. Allison and my family literally saved my life."

I opened my mouth to say something, but no words came out. "Jenny I...I don't know what to...say," I stuttered, then immediately broke into tears. Now I was the one sobbing while Jenny held me close. I felt like such an idiot. I was supposed to be comforting her, but I couldn't help it. The thought of Jenny going through that broke my heart.

"I'm sorry," I said, as I sat back and wiped my tears away. "I just can't believe you had to go through that. You're such an amazing person and it kills me that you were hurt like that. It's also a lot to wrap my head around. You're so much different than the girl you're describing."

"Does this..." Jenny hesitated before continuing. "...make you like me less?"

"I wish," I admitted with a laugh. "No, it makes me like you even more. You went through this awful time in your life, but you didn't let it break you. Instead you came out of it as this cool, confident, sexy as hell girl."

"It took a lot of work to become the person I am today. The rest of high school was pretty rough, but I was able to make it through with the help of my family and Allison's family. When I went to college, I used it as a completely fresh start. I didn't want to be the shy girl who gets taken advantage of and has her heart broken, so I put on this mask of fake confidence. Eventually, I actually started to feel the way I was pretending to feel."

"What about now? Are you truly happy?"

"I am," Jenny answered with a sincere smile. She followed it up with a yawn. "I'm exhausted though. Do you think we could get in bed?"

"Yeah…" I looked toward the bed that Jenny was already crawling into. "I can just sleep on the floor tonight. I don't want it to be weird now."

I started to turn around, but Jenny's hand wrapped around my wrist. "Will you please lay with me? Talking about that was really hard. It brought up a lot of emotions I haven't dealt with in a long time and...I...I need you."

She looked so sad and insecure that I would have done anything to take it away, so I crawled into the bed beside her, this time taking a spot more toward the center. Jenny backed into me and I wrapped my arms around her.

"Hey Jenny," I whispered into her ear. "I hope you know that I would never hurt you. I don't need any more from you than what you're willing to give me. What happened tonight doesn't have to change anything."

"Thank you Rory. That means a lot. I don't want anything to change." With those words, Jenny turned to me and took my face in her hands.

We both leaned in together and shared another kiss. This was different from the first one though. It was slow and delicate. I wasn't naive enough to believe it was the first of many kisses like this. No, this was different. This kiss was filled with promises and reassurance and I had a feeling it would be our last.

Chapter 16

Ryan waved at me eagerly as I pulled into the passenger pick up area of the Philadelphia airport. It was clear that he was just as excited about this little impromptu visit as I was. When he called me three weeks earlier and asked if I was free this weekend for a visit that Todd couldn't know about, I immediately knew what it was about. Ryan refused to give me any details aside from flight information. He also requested that I ask Todd's parents to get dinner the weekend he was coming, but not to tell them he would be there.

As soon as we were on the road heading back toward my hometown, I turned my eyes slightly toward him.

"Ok spill. We both know that I know exactly why you are coming here. So just say it. I can't wait any longer."

Ryan blatantly rolled his eyes at me. "Patience," he lectured. "I get to interrogate you first. So tell me, have you and Jenny kissed again?"

I rolled my eyes right back at him. "First of all, Jenny and I haven't seen each other for almost 8 months. It's kind of hard to kiss someone who is over 2000 miles away. Second of all, you know that we both agreed it was a one time thing."

"Hm I believe you mean two time thing," Ryan said with a smirk. "Have you forgotten about the slow, sensual bed make out."

I put one hand on my head, but couldn't suppress the laugh that left my mouth. "I so regret telling you and Todd about that. I don't know what we were thinking when we decided it was a good idea."

Ryan reached out and grabbed the hand that was holding my head. "You were thinking that you guys would need friends to talk about this with. Friends to ask you the tough questions. For example, have you thought about the fact that this is the longest you and Jenny have ever gone without seeing each other since you met? Do you think that has anything to do with the kiss?"

"Absolutely not," I lied. "We can't just fly across the country whenever we want. We still talk all the time. I can't remember the last time a day went by without us video chatting for at least an hour. Plus, we're constantly texting."

"But those are safe," Ryan interjected. "When you're across the country from each other, you know you won't accidentally slip up and kiss her again."

I groaned loudly. The truth was, Ryan was exactly right, but there was no way I would ever admit that. Things with Jenny were complicated, but I wasn't unhappy with where we were at. Although, I had to admit that I missed being in her presence terribly.

"Why don't you bother Jenny about this instead of me? Isn't *she* technically your bestie?" I was trying to throw it back at him, but I was also curious to see if he would slip up and give away how Jenny felt about the whole situation.

"Honey, that girl has so many walls, even Donald Trump is jealous. There's no way she's going to tell me anything."

Disappointed, I decided it was best to just change the subject. "Really though. Please just tell me what you flew all the way here to tell me."

"Ok," he said, taking a deep breath. "I was just wondering if it was ok if I asked your best friend to marry me."

———————————————

"Eeee," I squealed as we made our way up the walkway to Todd's parent's house. "I can't believe this is actually happening and I get to be part of it."

I jumped up and down while I took in Ryan's outfit again. He had taken forever to get ready once we were at my mom's house, claiming he had to look perfect. He was wearing new khaki pants with a white button up and blue tie. His long blonde hair was tamed as much as you could tame a Cali boy's mane. He was carrying flowers for Todd's Mom and a bottle of whiskey for his dad.

I knocked on the door and when Todd's Mom opened it, she went from looking excited to looking sincerely shocked.

"Ryan! What are you doing here?" She looked around and added, "Is Todd here too?"

"No, it's just me," Ryan said, running a hand through his hair. "Sorry to disappoint you."

Todd's mom threw a hand in the air. "Oh honey, stop that. You know I'm so happy to see you."

We waited by the door for Todd's Dad to come down and got pretty much the same reaction out of him. After the initial shock wore off, we got in the car to head to the Mexican restaurant I had made reservations at. I put my hand on Ryan's knee to try to keep it from bouncing up and down. He smiled appreciatively at me, but the bouncing didn't stop.

Once we were inside the restaurant and had ordered our food, Ryan took a deep breath and blew the air out slowly.

"So," he barely squeaked out before clearing his throat. "The reason I'm here... I have a very important question to ask you. Over the past three years, your son has become the most important part of my life. Todd is amazing in every way imaginable and I know so much of that has to do with you two. So I came here today because I was hoping...I was hoping I could have your blessing in asking your son to marry me."

Todd's Mom immediately broke into tears and even his dad looked like he was trying to hold back a few. He held out his hand for Ryan to shake. "There's nothing that would make us happier. We can't wait for you to officially be part of the family."

"There's one more thing," Ryan added. "I was hoping you would all come to California for the proposal."

Chapter 17

The two months leading up to the proposal dragged by. I didn't know if I was more excited to watch my best friend get engaged or to finally see Jenny again. I guess you could say I was also extremely nervous about the latter part. I didn't know how it would go after how we had left things the last time we saw each other.

The most nerve wracking part was that I had agreed to stay at Jenny's place and it would be just the two of us there. Since Todd's parents would be staying with him and Ryan, it would have been too crowded for me. I guess I could have stayed with my dad, but I must be a sucker for torture.

Once we landed and got our bags, Jenny picked us up and took us to her place to wait until it was time to join in on the proposal. Ryan was taking Todd back to the restaurant where we all went the first night they met. The plan was that Ryan was going to order them a dessert, but instead of bringing out the food, the restaurant was going to bring the ring box out on a plate. After he proposed, we were going to meet them there for actual dessert.

When Ryan texted that the proposal was about to occur, we all headed that way. Todd was shocked when we all walked in. He immediately showed us his ring which was a platinum band with each of their birthstones in it that Ryan had custom made.

"I wasn't sure how it worked with two guys," Todd's Dad admitted once we were sitting at the table. "I didn't know if you would propose with a ring or not."

Ryan explained that he really wanted the proposal to be as traditional as possible so he went the ring route. Todd added that the ring would serve as his wedding band too, but they were going to have it engraved with their wedding date once that time came.

When they were done explaining, Todd's Mom looked to me. "How do you think you'll do it when your big day comes Rory?"

I felt my whole face turning red. I had never told Todd's parents about my aversion to marriage. It's not exactly kosher in society these days to admit that you plan on dating around rather than ever settling down with someone. Except now I was starting to wonder if the dating around thing would even happen or if I would just be single for the rest of my life. Ever since Jenny and I kissed, any desire to date had completely gone away. If I was being completely honest with myself, dating hadn't been nearly as fun since I met Jenny since I compared every girl to her. But it was different now. I didn't want to date a girl that wasn't Jenny. I wasn't ready for the last kiss on my lips to be from anyone but her.

I came back from my thoughts and realized everyone at the table was now staring at me. "Oh sorry. I got caught up thinking about the question," I lied. "I guess if I were to get to that point with someone, I would want both of us to have engagement rings and then wedding bands. I think I would want to be the one to propose though."

I was saying "I think," but the truth was, I had actually thought about this. I was starting to think about things like this more and more lately.

Todd's mom turned her attention to Jenny, who seemed to be just a little too interested in my response for just a friend. "What about you sweetheart? Sorry for all the questions. I just find it so interesting since you guys don't have to go down the traditional route."

"Oh…" Jenny answered hesitantly. "I agree with Rory actually. If I ended up deciding marriage was the next step for me, I would want both of us to have the engagement rings and wedding bands. I would totally be all about having the bling to show off. I wouldn't want to be the one to propose though. That's way too much pressure."

Ryan leaned in and elbowed Todd's Mom. "She also thinks she's a queen, so proposing would totally be below her."

"Hey, if the tiara fits," Jenny said with a wink. I could tell she was uncomfortable with the conversation though. She gave me a reluctant smile and I naively wondered if we were both thinking the same thing. My mind was running away with crazy thoughts of what it would be like to propose to Jenny. I knew one thing for sure - she was the only person who could ever get me to rethink my stance on marriage. Except with her, I knew I wouldn't have to. Her reasons stemmed from much bigger issues than mine did and there was no way I could ever put her in a situation that would cause her the kind of pain she felt before.

After dinner, we said our goodbyes and headed back to Jenny's apartment. When I started to prepare the pull out couch, Jenny put a hand on my arm to stop me.

"Would you maybe consider sharing the bed with me?" She asked. She sounded unsure of herself, but then flirtatiously ran her fingers over my arm like she was confident in her decision. "I just love the feeling of these strong arms around me."

She stopped the trail of her fingers to squeeze my bicep and I sighed loudly, pushing her hand away. "You don't have to do that with me, you know."

"Do what?" Jenny asked innocently.

"Flirt to cover up your insecurities," I pointed out matter of factly.

Jenny made her face into a pout. "But I like to flirt. You know that. Don't try to contain my flirtation."

I couldn't help but smile at her. She was too cute to honestly be annoyed at. "I'm not going to lie, I also enjoy your flirtation. But we both know there are reasons that we shouldn't be crawling into bed together. And maybe it's for the best if we didn't sweep those reasons under the rug."

Jenny frowned slightly. "Listen Rory. I know you're right, but at this point, neither of us can deny how we feel about each other. We've both admitted to having feelings and although we haven't seen each other in months, I can tell you that my feelings haven't dwindled at all. And I'm going to guess by the way you're looking at me right now that yours haven't either. I understand why we agreed not to do that thing again that we also agreed not to talk about. It can lead to other things and we could end up getting hurt. There's no need to go down that road with the way...you...and I..we both... feel about commitment. But I like you Rory and I've missed having you close to me. I've missed being able to reach out and touch you. I've missed the feeling of your touch. And yeah, it might be absolute torture to cuddle close to each other and not be able to do anything else, but can you honestly think of any sweeter torture than that?"

"You know, if this whole movie business thing doesn't work out for you, maybe you should consider law school," I joked.

"So is that a yes?" Jenny asked excitedly.

Of course it was a yes. My answer would always be yes with Jenny. I didn't actually need convincing.

Once we were laying down, I wrapped my arms around her and I had to admit that it was indeed the sweetest torture. Nothing in this world could possibly feel better than Jenny's body up against mine. Ok, I take that back. Her lips on my lips was a pretty perfect feeling, but I willed myself not to think about that. I couldn't think about that. Not when we were this close. Not when I could easily get her to turn around and slowly bring our lips together, causing that explosion of feelings I hadn't been able to stop thinking about.

"Rory?" Jenny's voice interrupted my thoughts and I hoped she hadn't realized that my heart was now beating at a thousand miles per hour.

"Yeah?" I whispered, not able to get my voice to a normal volume.

"I was thinking…" My brain started moving even faster than my heartbeat. *What was she thinking? Was she*

ready for this to be more than what it already was? Was I?
"My boss has been on me about presenting a screenplay or documentary idea to him. I had an idea, but I don't know if I should do it. I wanted to make a documentary with lgbt individuals who are all different ages and from different demographic regions who came out in high school. I want to show the difference time periods and locations can make, but I also want to show anyone who might be struggling that it really does get better."

Even though that had taken a completely different direction than I expected, it was still exciting. I propped myself up on my elbow so I could look at Jenny. "Jenny I think that's an awesome idea. You have to do it and they would be stupid to not back you. When did you think of that?"

"I've actually been thinking about it for a long time," Jenny admitted. "It was kind of the reason I decided to go into film. I wanted to be able to make something like this that could make a difference to others like me. I didn't think I would ever be able to go through with it though. I wasn't brave enough until... until I met you."

I bent down and placed a kiss on Jenny's forehead, unsure what to say. Luckily, she spoke again before I had to.

"I always worried if I went through with a

documentary like this that it would bring up too many old feelings that I wouldn't be able to deal with. But now that I have you, I know that I can."

"You can and you will," I said softly as I took her hand and squeezed it.

My answer must have satisfied her because she relaxed back into me and shut her eyes. As my own eyes started to close, I wondered what the future with Jenny as my friend would be like if these feelings kept growing.

I was awoken early the next day to the sound of my phone ringing. I looked at the clock to find that it was just after 8 and wondered why someone would call me so early on a Saturday. Then I remembered that I was in California and for most of the people calling me it was already 11.

I picked up my phone and saw that it was my friend, Rebecca Thomas, calling. I thought it was strange that she would be calling since, aside from a few random texts here and there, I hadn't talked to her since she called to tell me she had gotten engaged. That was almost a year ago at this point.

"Hello?" I answered, trying not to give away the fact that the phone call had woken me up. Rebecca was one of the sweetest people ever so I knew she would feel bad about waking me.

"Hey Rory," she said cheerfully. "How are you?

What's new?"

"I'm good," I reported. "Nothing new here. Just living the dream."

I meant for it to be a joke, but as I looked over at Jenny still sleeping beside me, it really did feel like a dream.

"Good! I'm glad! Still living outside of Philly?"

"You bet. Are you still suffering through that small town life?"

Rebecca laughed at this. One thing we had bonded over early in our friendship was how much we both wanted to move on from our respective hometowns. That dream had changed drastically for Rebecca once she started dating her now fiancé, Cassie.

"On the contrast, I'd say that I'm actually living the dream too," she joked, but I knew it was sincere for her as well.

"So tell me. How is the wedding planning going?" I asked, excited to hear about what decisions they had made.

"It's going really well. We decided on a venue in Philadelphia. You know I can't completely let go of that city. The wedding is going to be in October. That's actually why I was calling. Could you text me your address? I know I could have just texted to ask, but it's been so long since we talked, I wanted to catch up. I was also wondering if you're seeing anyone. I wanted to make sure I gave you a plus one if you were."

I looked at Jenny again, who was starting to stir beside me and looked ridiculously cute with her hair and limbs all over the place.

"No… I'm not… dating anyone." It didn't feel right to say that I wasn't seeing anyone since the girl that I could see laying next to me didn't deserve to be completely denied.

Rebecca must have noticed my hesitation because she asked, "Is there someone special you would want to bring? It's ok if you're not actually dating."

"I definitely have someone… a… friend... I could bring. But don't feel like you have to give me a plus one. I know how expensive weddings are."

"Say no more. You're definitely getting a plus one. I'm intrigued now," Rebecca joked.

We talked about random subjects for the next ten minutes or so, then Rebecca told me she had to get going.

"By the way Rory. Here's some unsolicited advice from your older, wiser friend. Friends make the best lovers." She laughed and hung up before I could respond.

When I brought the phone away from my ear, Jenny blinked up at me, clearly having trouble opening her eyes.

"Who was that?" She asked, following her question

with a big yawn that wouldn't have looked nearly as adorable on anyone else.

"That was our excuse to see each other again. How would you feel about going to a wedding in Philadelphia in October?"

Jenny's eyes widened. "I think I better start working some overtime so I can get off a few days and really party it up. A wedding in Philadelphia sounds like fun."

"Plus, it's a lesbian wedding," I exclaimed. "That makes it even more exciting."

Jenny looked at me skeptically. "How did you say you know this person?"

"I didn't say," I teased. "She is a friend from college. She graduated two years ahead of me. And since I can tell you're wondering, no, we never dated. She was like a big sister to me; kind of took me under her wing in our college's lgbt club."

I saw Jenny's face relax a bit with this information. "Is it the typical lesbian love story? They met a month ago and now they are madly in love and getting married?"

"It's about the complete opposite of that," I chuckled. "They've been dating over five years I believe. But the best part is that they've known each other since they were kids. They were best friends growing up, lost touch, then came back together in their twenties and fell in love."

"Wow that's amazing," Jenny commented dreamily. "Sometimes I wish my past was different so I could believe that I could have a big love story like that."

"Yeah…" I lamented. *So do I…*

Chapter 18

The months leading up to Rebecca's wedding flew by. I went to California multiple times with the excuse that I was going to help with wedding plans since Todd and Ryan had picked a date in April. The truth was that I just wanted any excuse to see Jenny. Since I was Todd's "Best Woman" and Jenny was Ryan's, we decided to choreograph our reception entrance and worked on that more than we actually helped Todd and Ryan with wedding plans.

When the weekend of Rebecca's wedding came, I was excited for multiple reasons. Jenny was finally going to see my condo, I got to spend my weekend doing my favorite thing, and Jenny had told me a few weeks prior that she had big news for me, but wouldn't tell me until she saw me in person.

I picked Jenny up at the airport the morning of the wedding and took her back to my place to get ready. Since my condo had a guest bedroom and bathroom, we were able to get ready at the same time. I finished getting ready first and sat to watch tv while I waited for her. When she finally walked out of the guest room, I could feel my jaw drop. She was wearing a long red ball gown that was loose enough to be classy, but also left no secrets about her perfect curves.

Before meeting Jenny, I didn't know it was possible to constantly be blown away by someone, but this girl had the power to make me feel like I was seeing her for the first time every time.

I stood up and didn't try to hide my roaming eyes as they swept her body one more time.

"Jenny...Wow." My mouth felt dry and my head was spinning, so it was impossible to get any words out.

She took my hand and spun me around, taking in my floor length baby blue dress and licking her lips as she looked into my eyes. "Right back at you gorgeous."

I took her hand in mine, only letting go once we made it to my car. To my surprise, once I started driving, Jenny grabbed my free hand and wrapped her fingers back around mine. I wanted to ask her what we were doing, but I also didn't want to ruin the moment. I relished the feel of her touch, which made our half hour drive into the city seem much shorter.

We walked into the ballroom where the ceremony and reception were going to be and I lost my breath for the second time of the night. It was gorgeous. I couldn't imagine how much money Rebecca's family must have spent to get a place like this. The best part was the gorgeous chandelier in the middle of the room. Although the first thing to cross my mind was how the shimmer coming from the chandelier was nothing compared to Jenny's eyes.

We found our seats just in time for the ceremony to start. It was by far the most beautiful ceremony I had ever witnessed. I wasn't sure of the full story, but I knew that Rebecca and Cassie had full custody of Cassie's sister who seemed to be around 13. The ceremony was centered around the three of them officially becoming a family and the love radiating from all three of them was intoxicating. Caught up in the moment, I placed my hand on Jenny's knee. Before I could overthink it and move my hand away, Jenny's hand was on top of mine. We kept our hands like this, lost in the beauty of the moment. At some point, I twisted my hand around and intertwined my fingers with hers, only letting go when they brought our food out.

As soon as the DJ started playing, we headed out onto the dance floor. We laughed together as we tried to one up each other's ridiculous dance moves. For whatever reason, we were much more touchy this night. The touches were completely innocent, but they were constant. We were acting just like a couple - a very obsessed couple stuck in their honeymoon phase. The kind of couple that I would have made fun of in the past. But in this moment, I didn't care. It felt good to act this way with Jenny and that's all that mattered. I could worry about what it all meant later. For now, I was just going to enjoy myself.

When the music switched to a slow song, I pulled Jenny as close to me as possible. She laid her head gently on my shoulder as we swayed along to the music. My mind wandered to what it would be like if this were actually my life; if I could hold Jenny close whenever I wanted. I wanted her close all the time. I didn't want to think about her being back across the country so I chased those thoughts from my mind. When the song ended, we both continued to hold on to each other until the moment was broken up by a very drunk guy bumping into us.

We danced for a few more songs, then went to the DJ booth to request a High School Musical song. Along with choreographing the entrance for the boys' wedding, we had also spent the past few months learning the dances to most of the songs from all three High School Musical movies. Once the song came on, we broke into the dance and quickly drew quite the crowd. We both grabbed random people and began teaching them the dance and by the end of the song most of the wedding guests were doing some rendition of the dance. Granted, it looked terrible, but everyone seemed to be having a good time at least. Once the song was over, Jenny leaned in close to whisper in my ear.

"I'm going to take a potty break," she declared, before taking off.

I looked around the room and found Rebecca just a few feet away from me. When I was by her side, I pulled her into an embrace and told her how beautiful the wedding was.

"Thank you," she said, looking around to take everything in. "It really is so much better than I could have dreamed of. So, where is your girl?"

"Potty break," I informed her, not bothering to correct the fact that she called Jenny my girl. "Not going to lie, I don't think I've ever seen anyone as in love as you and Cassie. It's really beautiful."

Rebecca looked toward Cassie dreamily. "Yeah, Cass is my everything. I love her and Katie more than anything in this world. Love is funny that way." I nodded but looked past her toward Jenny who had just walked back into the ballroom. I followed her with my eyes as Rebecca continued to speak, taking in the words as if they were about Jenny. "If you would have told me ten years ago that I was going to get back in touch with Cassie and the two of us would fall madly in love, I would have said you were crazy. She was a distant memory for so long and suddenly she was everything. You live your life without someone for so long and then after being in your life for a short time, you can't even remember what life was like before them. Everything becomes about them and how they make you feel. The past is suddenly so unimportant because life without this person isn't living at all."

Rebecca's eyes followed mine to Jenny who was now standing right beside us. "But I'd say it looks like you know exactly how I feel." She reached out her hand to shake Jenny's. "It's so nice to meet you finally. Sorry it's been so crazy here tonight."

Jenny told her it was fine and the two of them spent the next ten minutes getting to know each other better. Rebecca then apologetically told us that she should go talk to some other guests. I took this as an opportunity to ask Jenny if she was ready to head back to my place. I didn't want to risk being sleepy on the drive back. Jenny held her hand out to me and we walked to my car hand in hand, again continuing to hold hands for the whole drive home.

Once we had changed into comfier clothes, Jenny asked if I was ready to hear her big news, lifting her eyebrows as a tease.

"Of course I want to hear," I said impatiently.

She took a deep breath. "You know how I submitted my documentary idea a little while back? They accepted it. Rory, I'm going to make a documentary. It's really happening."

Once her words registered, I couldn't contain my excitement. I picked her up and twirled her around, putting her feet back on the ground only to pull her into a tight hug. We both held on longer than necessary and somewhere in the middle of the hug, our demeanor changed. It was no longer a congratulatory hug. It was a hug of desperation, with both of us sinking further into each other.

When we finally pulled back, we continued holding onto each other's arms. Jenny stared into my eyes and I felt like she was looking right through to my soul. I used my hand to move a stray piece of hair behind her ear and when I did, I heard Jenny gasp. I kept my hand behind her ear and continued to stare at her, completely lost in the moment.

I looked down toward her mouth, contemplating whether I should just lean in and kiss her. Every single ounce of my body was begging me to. Jenny looked from my eyes to my lips then back up again.

She opened and closed her mouth a few times like she was trying to say something but didn't know how to get the words out.

"Jenny…" I whispered trying to form a coherent thought, but at that moment Jenny said the words she had been trying to say.

"I haven't stopped thinking about that kiss since the night it happened"

Before I had time to think, our lips were crashing together. The kiss was everything I had dreamed about for the past year, but at the same time, it was so much better.

This time, instead of just letting our mouths do the work, our hands started moving over each other's bodies as well. I moved my hands up and down Jenny's sides, while she reached out and gripped onto my backside through my sweatpants.

I kissed my way down her neck and across her collarbone, while she threw her head back in pleasure. When she brought her face back up toward mine she nibbled on my ear, causing me to let out a low growl.

"Rory," she begged. "I need you."

I didn't need to hear anything more. I picked her up and carried her into my room, gently laying her on the bed and crawling on top of her. We slowly removed layer by layer of each other's clothes, taking the time to soak up every moment. Once we were completely naked, I stopped what I was doing to sweep my eyes over Jenny's body and completely take her in.

That's when it hit me. I loved this girl. I was in love with Jennifer Anneliese Hanson and I wanted to show it in the most intimate way possible.

Chapter 19

I opened my eyes the next day to find Jenny asleep on my chest. From the lack of clothes, I was able to deduce that the night before hadn't been a dream. I had fantasized about a night like this with Jenny multiple times, but I always worried that I would regret it if it actually happened. But laying here with her, running my hands through her hair while I watched her sleep, I didn't regret anything. I wanted more. I found myself excited for her to wake up so I could finally tell her how I felt.

When I felt her start to stir, I bent down and placed a gentle kiss on her lips. She opened her eyes and smiled up at me.

"Hey there pretty girl. Did you get a good night's sleep?" I asked.

She wrapped her arms around my waist to pull me close. "The best."

We laid like this for a few minutes, until I willed myself to sit up. Jenny sat up beside me, the grin never leaving her face.

"So, I think we should talk about what happened last night and what it means for us in the future." My grin grew wider as I said the words, but I noticed that Jenny's smile started to slip.

Soon her whole face was pale and a scared look appeared. Except she didn't just look scared. She looked terrified. My heart felt like it dropped out of my chest. My worst nightmares were coming true. She didn't want this. Of course she didn't. Why did I ever start to make myself believe that she did?

I continued to watch her as she said nothing, but I could have sworn she was on the brink of tears. I couldn't stand to see her like this. I knew I had to make things easier on her, even if it made my life a thousand times harder.

"Maybe we should just forget this ever happened...if that's what you want." The words left a sour taste in my mouth. There would be no forgetting what had happened last night.

I watched Jenny expectantly, hoping she would fight back. I wanted her to tell me that it's not what she wanted, but instead her words stung more than I could have imagined. "Yeah. I think that's for the best."

My heart broke instantly, but I promised myself I wouldn't cry. I couldn't let her see me like that. I wanted her to be happy and I knew she couldn't be if she knew I was upset. The day passed by slowly with each of us trying to act as normal as possible and failing miserably.

When it was time to go to bed for the night, Jenny headed to the guest room without saying anything. I cried myself to sleep wondering how something so beautiful could make everything so bad.

The next day, I woke up early to drive Jenny to the airport. We barely spoke the whole trip, but held each other close before saying goodbye. We promised that we would text and video chat every day and that we would see each other again before the wedding day, but even the promises felt empty.

In one of the conversations we did have, we decided not to tell anyone what had happened, especially not Todd and Ryan. The next few months were the loneliest months of my life. You know the part in the second Twilight movie when Bella is heartbroken and spends months just staring out the window? The part that seems so dramatic and unrealistic to anyone who has never gone through it? I felt like that was my life. I felt like an empty shell of a person just watching the world pass me by.

Jenny and I kept our promises to try to keep in touch, but it only made things harder. Our conversations were nothing like they were in the past and we both came up with excuses to skip out on skype or FaceTime. Although I felt guilty about it, I found excuses not to travel to California to help Todd with wedding plans. The one time I did fly out there for a few days, Jenny and I somehow avoided seeing each other. I realized it was pretty easy to avoid someone when they were avoiding you too.

A few weeks before the wedding, I couldn't take it anymore. I knew Jenny and I were going to be spending a lot of time together on the wedding weekend and the boys didn't deserve for us to make it awkward.

The day I called her, she surprisingly picked up after just two rings, immediately asking me if everything was ok. That was the thing with Jenny. I knew no matter how bad it got between us, she would never stop caring and that alone kept me hanging on.

"I'm ok," I tried to lie. "No I'm not. Everything sucks right now Jenny. As much as I don't want to admit it, nothing is the same between us."

Jenny sighed. "I know. I'm not sure how we could expect it to stay the same though."

"What are we going to do?" I knew I wasn't hiding the desperation in my voice, but there was no use to try. I was desperate.

"I don't know Ror," Jenny answered a little too truthfully. "But I do think this is something we should talk about in person."

I reluctantly agreed and suffered through the next few weeks leading up to the wedding weekend.

The day I arrived in LA was much too busy to get any time alone with Jenny. We both tried our best to act cordial toward each other and act like nothing was wrong.

The morning of the wedding, I knew I had to suck it up and talk to her. I woke up early and headed to her hotel room, taking a deep breath before knocking on the door. When Jenny opened up, she looked surprised to see me, but asked me to come in.

We both sat on her bed in silence for a few minutes. All I could think about was what had happened the last time we were in bed together.

"Please tell me what to do to make things better between us." Jenny jumped at my words, surprised to hear me break the silence.

I tried to take her hand in mine, but she grabbed it away from me like I was a stranger.

"Could you just tell me what I did wrong?" I asked.

"Seriously Rory?" Jenny scoffed.

I guess it was a pretty dumb question to ask. I knew exactly what I had done wrong. I had broken our one promise to each other.

"I'm sorry I had sex with you. I should have stopped

it from happening." Except that was a lie. I wasn't sorry. It was the most passionate night of my life and I regretted nothing about it, except the aftermath.

"That's honestly what you're apologizing for right now?" I could tell by Jenny's voice that she was frustrated, but I didn't know what she wanted from me.

"Yes? No? Ugh I don't know. I'm just trying to make things right here."

I tried to look to Jenny for answers, but she had completely shut down on me. I waited a few minutes then without saying anything, I stood and headed for the door.

"I was falling in love with you." Jenny's words caused my hand to drop from the door.

I turned around to find her staring at me with tears streaking her cheeks.

"Wh-what?" I stammered, feeling like the wind had been knocked out of me.

"I think I was falling for a long time, but it wasn't until the night of Rebecca's wedding that I realized that the feelings I was having went so far beyond a stupid crush. I had to pull away Rory. It was too hard knowing that what happened between us meant so much more to me than it meant to you."

My head was spinning. I felt like I was going to pass

out. I placed my hand on a nearby wall to keep myself upright. "Jenny what happened between us...it meant everything to me. It's all I've thought about since that night. My heart feels whole and broken at the same time because it was the best and worst thing to ever happen to me. Walking away the next morning when all I wanted to do was give my whole heart to you was the hardest thing I've ever done. I didn't want that. I didn't want any of this. I wanted you."

Jenny's face contorted in a way that I couldn't read. She looked angry, sad, and shocked all at the same time and it was like her body couldn't decide which emotion was going to win out.

"But y-y-you. Why Rory? Why are you just saying this now? You said... *YOU* said.. that we should forget it happened. I didn't want that. God Rory... for the first time in my life, I was ready to face my fears. I wanted us to be more. Why would you say that we should forget everything that happened if you didn't really want to forget?"

I stumbled back over to her bed, grasping my stomach as I sat down. I felt like I was going to be sick. "Shit Jenny... I said that because I thought you wanted it. I wanted to make it easier on you. You looked so scared."

Jenny sat down next to me and rested her head against mine. "Of course I looked scared. I was about to give my heart to someone. The last time I did that, my world fell apart."

"Damnit Jenny." I punched my fist against the bed. I wasn't mad at her and I wanted her to know that, but I couldn't get my thoughts straight. "I said that we could forget it if that's what *YOU* wanted and *you* said it was for the best."

With those words, I began sobbing and buried my head into Jenny's shoulder. To my surprise, she pulled me closer. I was repeating the word sorry over and over again, unsure if she could actually hear me through the sobs and the muffling by her own shirt.

"Shh," she soothed. "I'm sorry too. I'm so sorry. We both messed up. We're both so so bad at this. We had something beautiful and we... we ruined it."

I pulled back, wiping the tears from my face. "B-but it's not too late. We can still make things better. I still feel the same way. Nothing has changed."

Jenny sighed. "Everything has changed Ror. We hurt each other. We promised we never would and we did."

"But we can make it better. I can make it better." I knew I was begging now, but I couldn't control myself. My world was slipping out from under me.

"I wish we could," Jenny whispered, with a sadness to

her voice that I had never heard before. "It doesn't make sense Rory. We don't even live in the same state. Neither of us is willing to move. It's unrealistic to think we could somehow make this work."

I felt my whole body deflate and any segments of my heart that still remained shattered on the spot. There was nothing I could say. I couldn't fight that. She was right. I didn't want her to be right, but she was.

We grabbed onto each other and held on tight, crying in each other's arms. It was beautiful and tragic all at once. That's what Jennifer Anneliese Hanson and I were - a beautiful tragedy.

_____-

"So are you ready?" I looked over to see Jenny's big brown eyes already staring at me. Those were the eyes that first attracted me to her and they still had the habit of taking my breath away, even though I knew they shouldn't. Her eyes always had such a nice shimmer to them, only today they didn't. Today they just looked sad. It killed me to see them looking that way. All I wanted to do was reach out and grab her hand. I wanted to tell her that everything would be ok. I wanted to promise that we would find a way to make things better. More than anything, I just wanted to make her smile again.

Instead I shrugged my shoulders and forced a fake smile onto my face. I threw on a pair of sunglasses and as the music started, I took her hand and broke into our choreographed entrance, hoping no one would realize just how broken up I was inside.

Our entrance was somehow flawless. To the outside world, we were perfect. But we both knew that we were broken. The only thing that was making me happy was the fact that I hadn't found a way to mess up Todd's big day.

While we sat at the head table, just feet away from each other, I willed myself not to look at Jenny. I knew if I looked at her I would break down again. It didn't matter if everyone in the room saw. There was no way I would be able to control it. I felt a hand grab mine and looked up to see Todd staring at me.

"It's time for your toast." He nodded his head toward the DJ who was standing by me with a microphone. "Are you ok to do this?"

I nodded my head. The fact that he would even ask that on the day that was supposed to be all about him just proved that I owed him this. Luckily I made it through without having a breakdown. After I finished, both Todd and Ryan stood to hug me and it took everything in me to let go.

I tuned out while Jenny gave her speech. It might

seem dramatic, but I couldn't bear to hear her voice. The rest of the night went by in a blur. I danced and drank, doing anything I could to keep my mind off of Jenny which proved to be hard as we kept stealing glances at each other from across the room.

The night ended with me drunkenly tucking myself into bed and crying myself to sleep. I knew it wasn't my best moment, but I couldn't bring myself to care.

The next day I awoke to a knock at my door. I jumped out of bed, hope surging through me. I tried to mask my disappointment when I opened the door to find Todd standing in front of me. He pushed past me into my room and sat on my bed.

"Ok, I'm just going to be straight with you. You look awful right now." He sniffed the air and turned his nose up. "You don't smell so good either. It smells like sweaty vodka in here."

When I didn't crack a smile at his jokes, Todd patted the spot on the bed next to him. "Talk to me. What's up? What's going on with you and Jenny?"

"Well, the truth is..." I hesitated for a moment, unsure if I should tell him. "Jenny and I had sex."

A smile spread across Todd's face and he slapped the bed with the palm of his hand. "Well hot damn. It's about time. Is that what the smell is in here? I thought maybe it was a sex smell. Was it make up sex from whatever issue you guys have clearly been having the past few months? Where is Jenny? Hiding in the closet? Come on you have to..."

"Todd please." I put up a hand to signal him to stop talking. "We didn't just have sex. We had sex at the last wedding we went to."

Todd looked toward the ceiling and started raising his fingers like he was counting something. "But that was six months ago. Why wouldn't you tell me?"

I shrugged. "You and Ryan were busy planning your wedding. This is the happiest time of your lives. We didn't want to do anything to ruin that."

Todd placed his hand on my knee. "But you guys are our best friends. We care about you so much more than we care about some dumb wedding."

His eyes burned into me. "You really should have told me. So the sex… is that what caused your problems?"

I nodded my head then went through the whole story, starting with Rebecca's wedding and ending with the confessions from the morning before.

After I was done, Todd exhaled loudly like he had been holding his breath the whole time.

"You have to do something Ror," he ordered. "I've

been telling you from the beginning that you guys were meant to be together. It can't end like this."

"It's too late. It's just too late." My shoulders dropped as I said the words.

We both looked toward the door when we heard a knock. Todd patted me on the knee and stood up.

"That's probably Ryan wondering where I'm at. I'll get it."

When the door opened, it wasn't Ryan standing on the other side, but Jenny instead. Todd gave her a hug, then excused himself.

Jenny walked over to the bed and sat beside me, taking my hand and laying her head on my shoulder. We sat like this for a few minutes before Jenny broke the silence.

"Do you think we can try to be friends again?"

"Jenny, no matter what, I'll always be your friend," I answered sincerely.

Jenny sighed. "I know that. But I mean can we try to go back to how we were before? I know it won't be easy, but I need that. I need you."

"I'll try my best, but it's not going to be easy," I admitted.

Jenny nodded her head and we sat in silence again. Neither of us said another word but the air between us seemed to be full of promises that I hoped and prayed we could actually keep this time.

After awhile, I walked Jenny to the door and we shared a long hug. I watched as she walked away and for the first time since becoming friends, I wondered if I would ever see Jenny Hanson again.

Chapter 20

After I landed in Pennsylvania and packed my luggage in my car, I started my trip. I drove right past the exit for my condo and stayed on the road for another two hours. When I arrived at my destination, I knocked loudly on the door, collapsing into open arms as soon as the door opened.

"Mommy," I cried into her shoulder. No matter how old I got I would never be too old to need my mom and this was one of those times.

My mom directed me into the house and sat me down on the couch, taking the seat beside me. She rubbed my back while I sobbed, letting out all of my pent up feelings from the past few months; heck, from the past few years.

"What's going on Rory? Is this about Jenny?"

I nodded through my sobs, not questioning how my mom knew that. Moms had a way of knowing everything.

"I was happy before I met Jenny. I felt whole. I thought I had it all. And then I met her and she made me feel things I've never felt before and I realized that there was this happiness that I didn't even think was possible. But a lot has happened and now everything is a mess and I feel like a part of me is missing and I don't know how I'm ever supposed to be whole again without her."

"Well the solution is pretty simple," my mom said nonchalantly while wiping the tears from my eyes. "Don't live without her."

"That's the goal, but there are too many feelings involved now. I don't want to live as just her friend. I'm not sure if I can."

"Well, are these feelings mutual?" My Mom asked, clearly trying to make the situation seem much more simple than it actually was.

"I think they are. No, I know they are."

My mom stared at me for a few minutes like she was trying to figure out where the problem was, but then a sad look of realization entered her face. "Is this about your father and I? You're not trying to avoid a relationship to avoid ending up like us are you? Because you can't live like that Rory. You can't expect things to turn out the way they did for us. Your father and I were so young when we got together. When we first started dating, we really did love each other, but somewhere along the line we didn't feel the love anymore, we just felt comfortable together. When we were at the point where we should have ended things, we were also at the age when people expected us to get married and have kids. So we did what was expected. I thought I could be happy with your father because we really did care about each other, but because there was no love, we grew to resent each other and that resentment manifested itself as hatred."

By the time my mom finished, she had tears in her eyes and all I wanted to do was make her feel better. "I'm going to be honest. That's how it started out. That's why I never got into any serious relationships and why I decided that Jenny and I couldn't be together. But that's not the case anymore. I would take the risk for her."

"Then what's the problem?"

"We live on different ends of the country Mom. We can't exactly just drive down the street to see each other. Plus, I don't think she trusts that I won't hurt her."

"Then move to her. Prove to her that you would do anything to be together. Show up at her apartment and tell her how you feel about her."

My mom's words shocked me. Weren't parents supposed to be the rational ones? Weren't they supposed to lecture us kids about not making life altering decisions on a whim.

"So, let me get this straight," I reiterated. "You want me to pack up my whole life and move across the country just for some girl that might not even want to hear what I have to say?"

"Is Jenny really just some girl?"

"No, she isn't. I'm madly in love with her mom. But let's say I did do something crazy like move out there. What if I spill my heart out to her and she still doesn't want to be with me?"

My mom laughed at this. "I highly doubt that will happen. I've seen the way she looks at you. She wants to be with you just as much as you want to be with her. Plus, it's not like you would be moving out there JUST for her. You love LA. The first time we ever vacationed there when you were just a kid, you told me that you were going to move there someday. You talked about it all through high school too. I was shocked when you told me you were moving out to go live near Philly. It never added up."

"I can't move to LA mom. I can't leave you. I'm not choosing Dad over you. He doesn't deserve that. *You* don't deserve that."

My mom pulled me into her, embracing me from the side. "Oh honey. Is that really what you're afraid of? Do you think if you move to LA that I'll think you chose your father over me? I would never think that. You don't have to choose between us. The only choice you need to make is what is going to make you happy."

I considered her words. "Jenny makes me happy

mom. California makes me happy too. But I can't imagine being so far away from you that I couldn't just drive a few hours to see you. You're my best friend. I don't think I can leave you."

My mom stared at me for a few seconds like she was trying to think of the right motherly advice to give me, but then her face lit up like she had just come up with the greatest idea of all time.

"What if you could have it all?" She asked. "What if I came with you? I know it sounds crazy, but there's really nothing keeping me here now that your grandparents are both gone. I can get a job anywhere."

I looked into my mom's eyes, wondering if it was a mom thing to be this crazy or if it was just my mom. "You would really do that for me?"

"Honey, I would do anything for you."

———————

Once my mom made up her mind about something, she worked quickly. She immediately put her house up for sale and began packing things up. Luckily, we got an offer on the house pretty quickly and my mom agreed to come to LA as soon as everything was settled. Since I was renting my condo, I paid the landlord extra money to break my lease early.

I started looking at houses that my mom and I could share until she found one of her own. By the time I was ready to head to LA, I had a few places that I was considering. I know I could have waited until I officially had a place to head to LA, but I had waited long enough to be with Jenny and I had the perfect plan to win her over, but it involved being there in June.

When I arrived in Los Angeles, rainbows were everywhere. They really did go all out for their pride festival. I dropped my bags off at Ryan and Todd's apartment, reminding Todd exactly where he and Jenny should be standing on the parade route and then went to meet Ryan at his nonprofit.

On the way, I sent Jenny a text telling her to have fun at pride. I knew she would question if I didn't text her since we had both been working really hard to restore our friendship.

I smiled as I walked into the Unicorn Cove and read the text Jenny had sent me.

I wish you were here with me. Could you please plan a trip to California soon?

"Someone's happy today," Ryan said as he walked up

to me and kissed my cheek. "It's so good to see you again Rory. I'm so excited for today."

"I'm extremely anxious," I admitted. "What if it's not enough?"

Ryan chuckled, throwing his head back. "Girl. You planned a whole move across the country in just two months so you could confess your love during pride. It's more than enough. Plus, it's Jenny. You could have confessed your love over the phone and it would have been enough. She's mad about you."

"Thanks Ryan and thank you for doing all of this for me. I feel bad that you changed your whole float theme just to accommodate me."

"Stop that," he said with a flick of the wrist. "High School Musical is a great theme. I don't care if half the kids here are too young to appreciate it and the other half think they are too cool for it. One thing we can all agree on is the fact that Zac Efron is sexy."

We joined some of the regulars from the Unicorn Cove and walked with them to the beginning of the parade route where our float was waiting for us. The float looked awesome in person. It was red and white and had "East High Wildcats" written on the side. The best part was the speaker system that was going to blast the soundtrack as we made our way through the parade route.

When we were about halfway through the parade route, we came up on the area where I had told Todd to stand with Jenny.

Ryan handed me a megaphone and patted me on the back. "Are you ready for this?"

I didn't say anything because I honestly wasn't sure if I was ready. That was until I looked into the crowd and saw her. She was wearing a rainbow crop top and short jean shorts. There was glitter on her face and her tan arms were covered with rainbow tattoos. She looked stunning. As I looked at her, everyone else disappeared.

I held the megaphone up to my mouth and started to speak. "Jennifer Anneliese Hanson. I need to talk to you."

When she turned to look in my direction, the sun reflected off of her eyes and they shimmered in the same way they did the first day I met her. I was so captivated that I almost forgot what I had come to say. But the shocked smile on her face encouraged me to continue.

"I had this whole speech planned out, but now as I'm looking at you, I can't seem to remember any of it. So I'm just going to say it. I love you Jenny. I'm madly in love with you. So much so that I moved across the country on the off chance that you would forgive me."

I jumped off of the float and ran up to her since I didn't want to say the next part through a megaphone for everyone to hear. When I was beside her, I took both of her hands in mine.

"That night that we finally let go and gave ourselves to one another was the best night of my life. It was the night that I realized just how much I loved you. But the months that followed were the worst. They showed me how empty my life is without you. I'm not going to stand here and promise to never hurt you because I know that's not realistic. A relationship isn't going to be easy. It isn't going to be perfect. We're both going to make a lot of mistakes. But, my God, will it be worth it. Please tell me that it's worth it to you too."

Jenny beamed while shaking her head at me. "Of course it's worth it. You're worth it. I love you too Rory. I love you so much."

With that, she leaned in and kissed me. We kissed like there was no one else around and I honestly forgot there was until I heard the hoots and hollers, the loudest ones of course coming from Todd and Ryan.

We both broke into laughter as we stared into each other's eyes. Jenny removed her hand from mine, placing her pointer finger on my chin dimple.

"I love you Miss Montgomery."

"I love you too Jenny wedding."

THE END